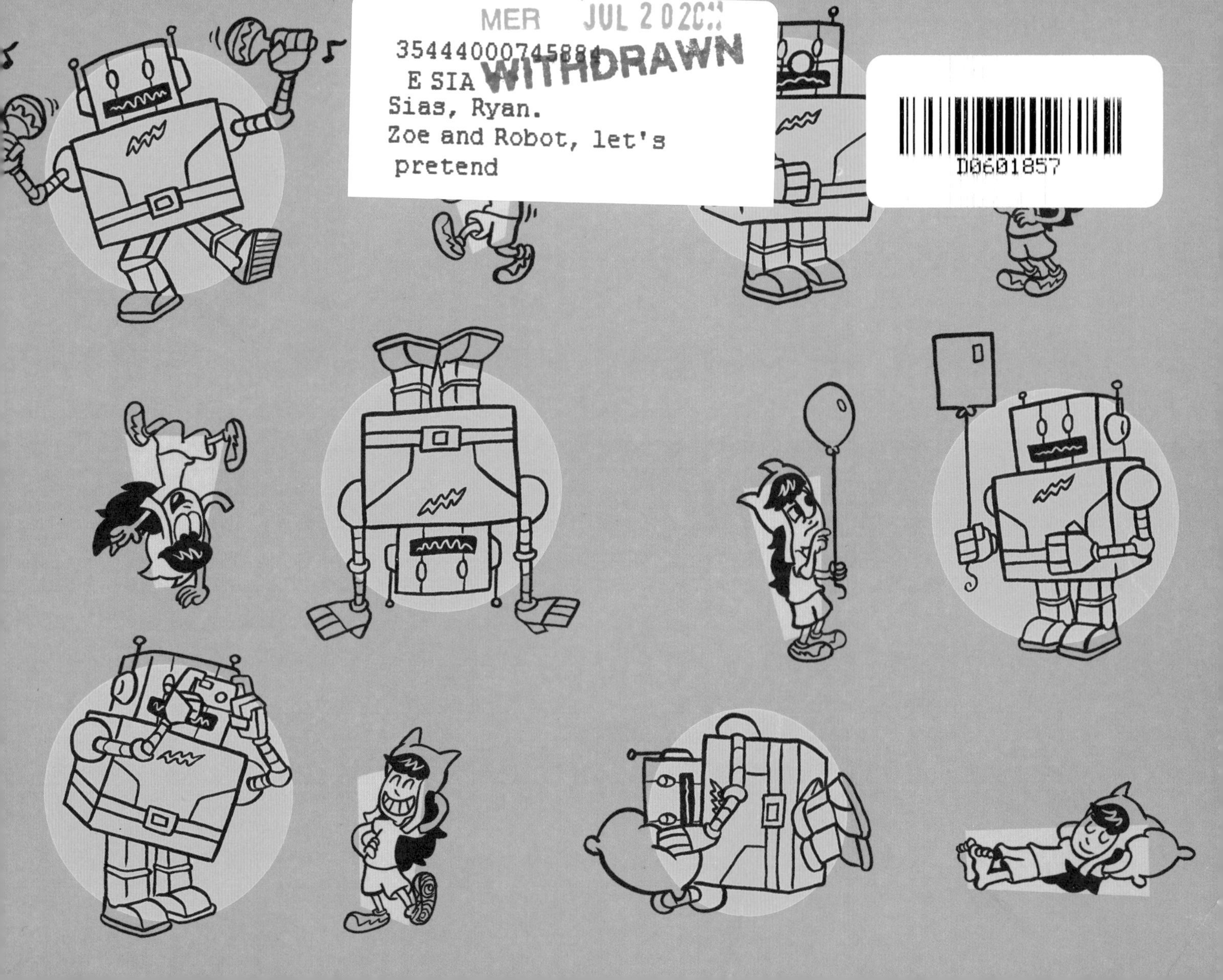

Copyright ©2011 Ryan Sias
Balloon Toons™ is a registered
trademark of Harriet Ziefert, Inc.
All rights reserved/CIP data is available.
Published in the United States 2011 by
🍎 Blue Apple Books
515 Valley Street, Maplewood, NJ 07040
www.blueapplebooks.com

First Edition
Printed in China 03/11
ISBN: 978-1-60905-063-4

2 4 6 8 10 9 7 5 3 1

BALLOON TOONS™

Ryan Sias

Zoe AND Robot

Let's Pretend!

🍎 BLUE APPLE BOOKS

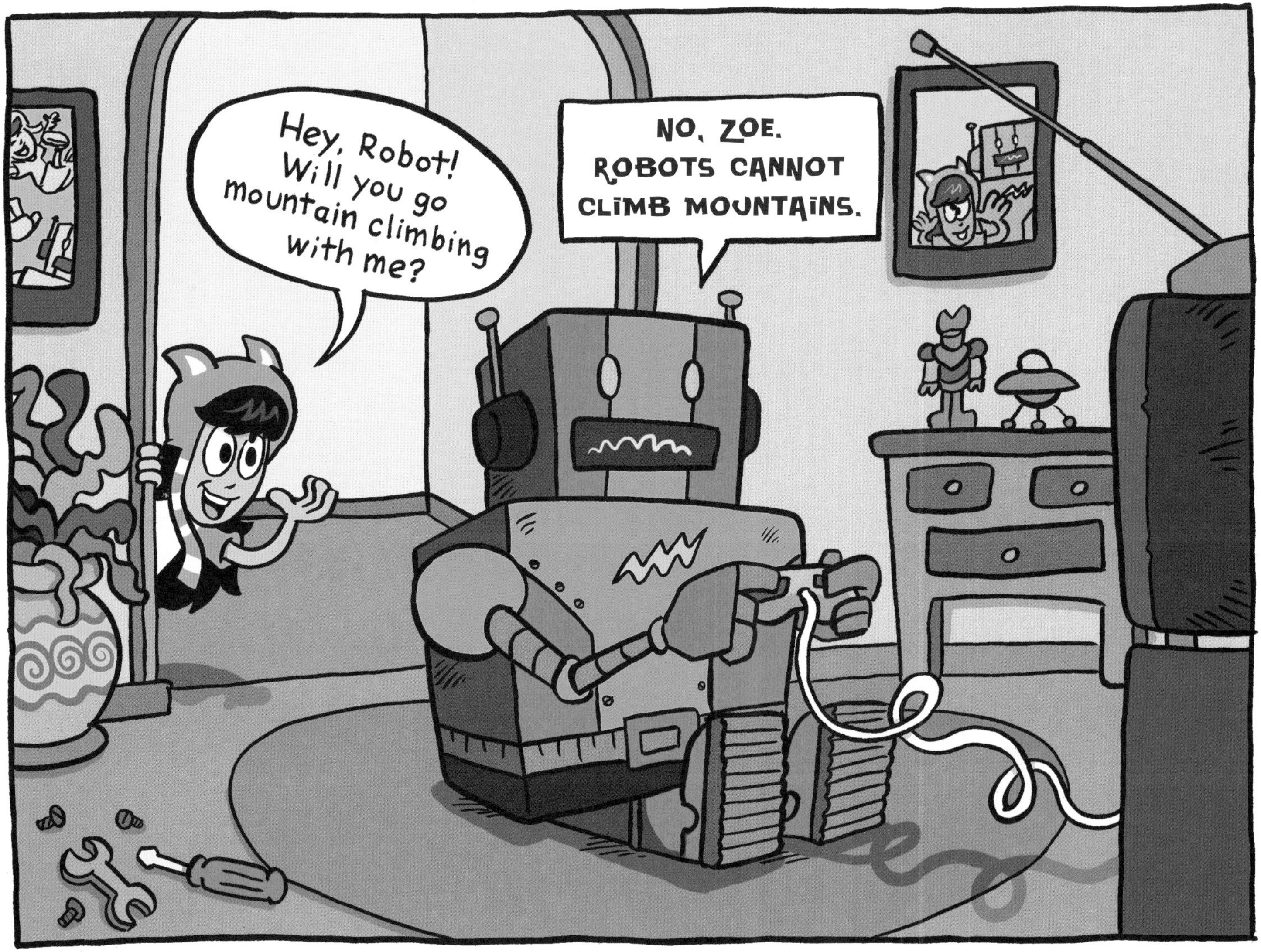
Hey, Robot! Will you go mountain climbing with me?
NO, ZOE. ROBOTS CANNOT CLIMB MOUNTAINS.

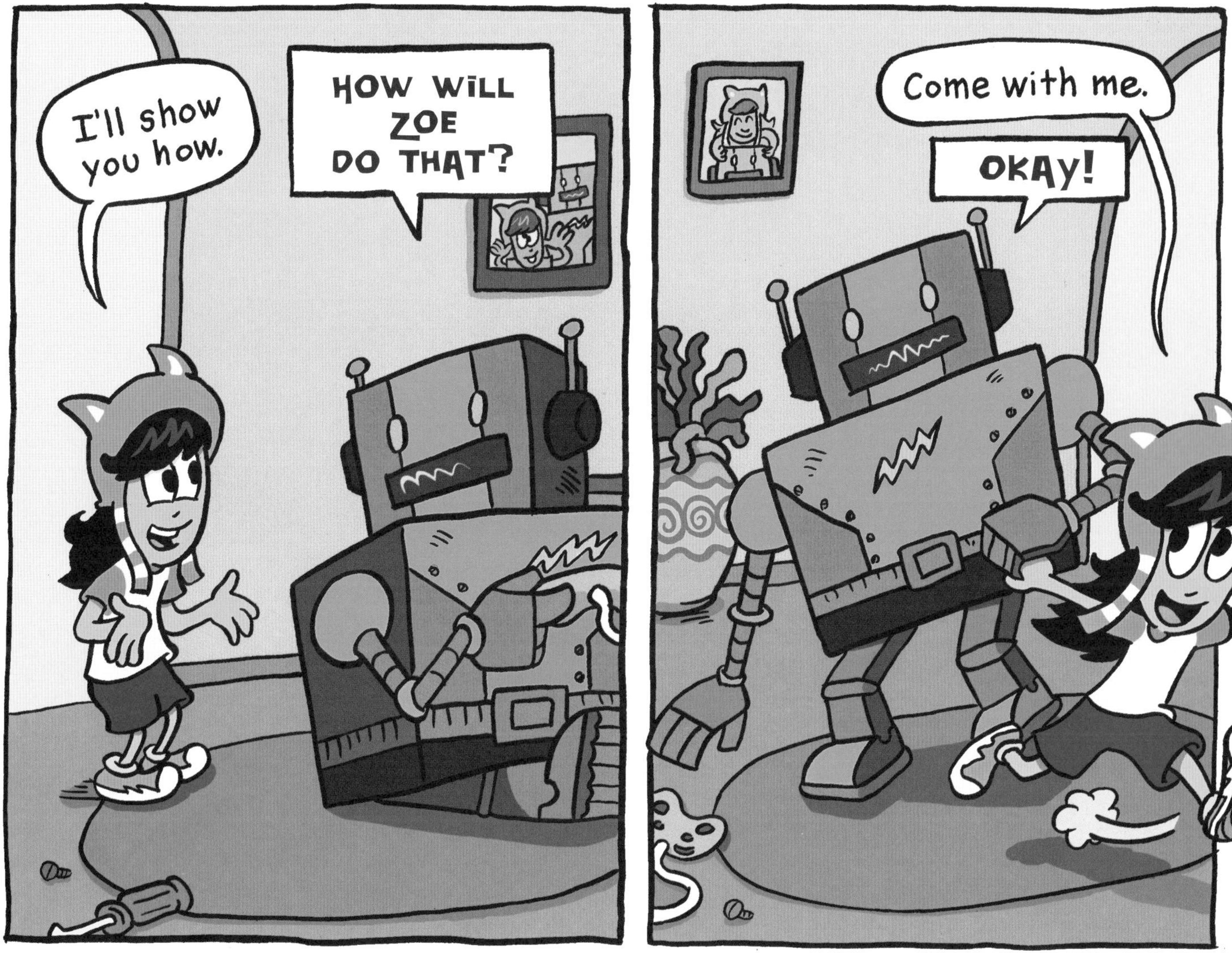
I'll show you how.
HOW WILL ZOE DO THAT?
Come with me.
OKAY!

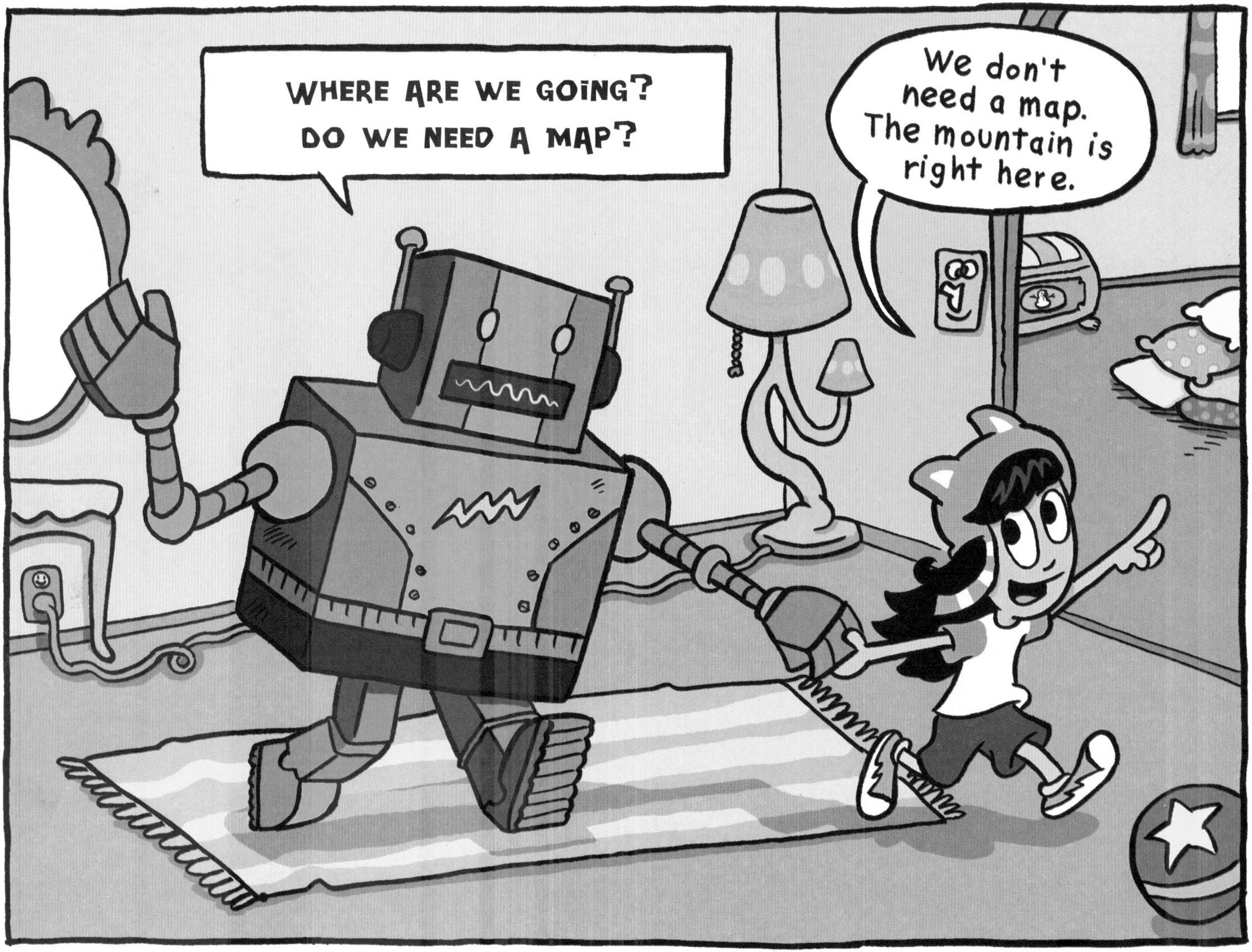
WHERE ARE WE GOING? DO WE NEED A MAP?
We don't need a map. The mountain is right here.

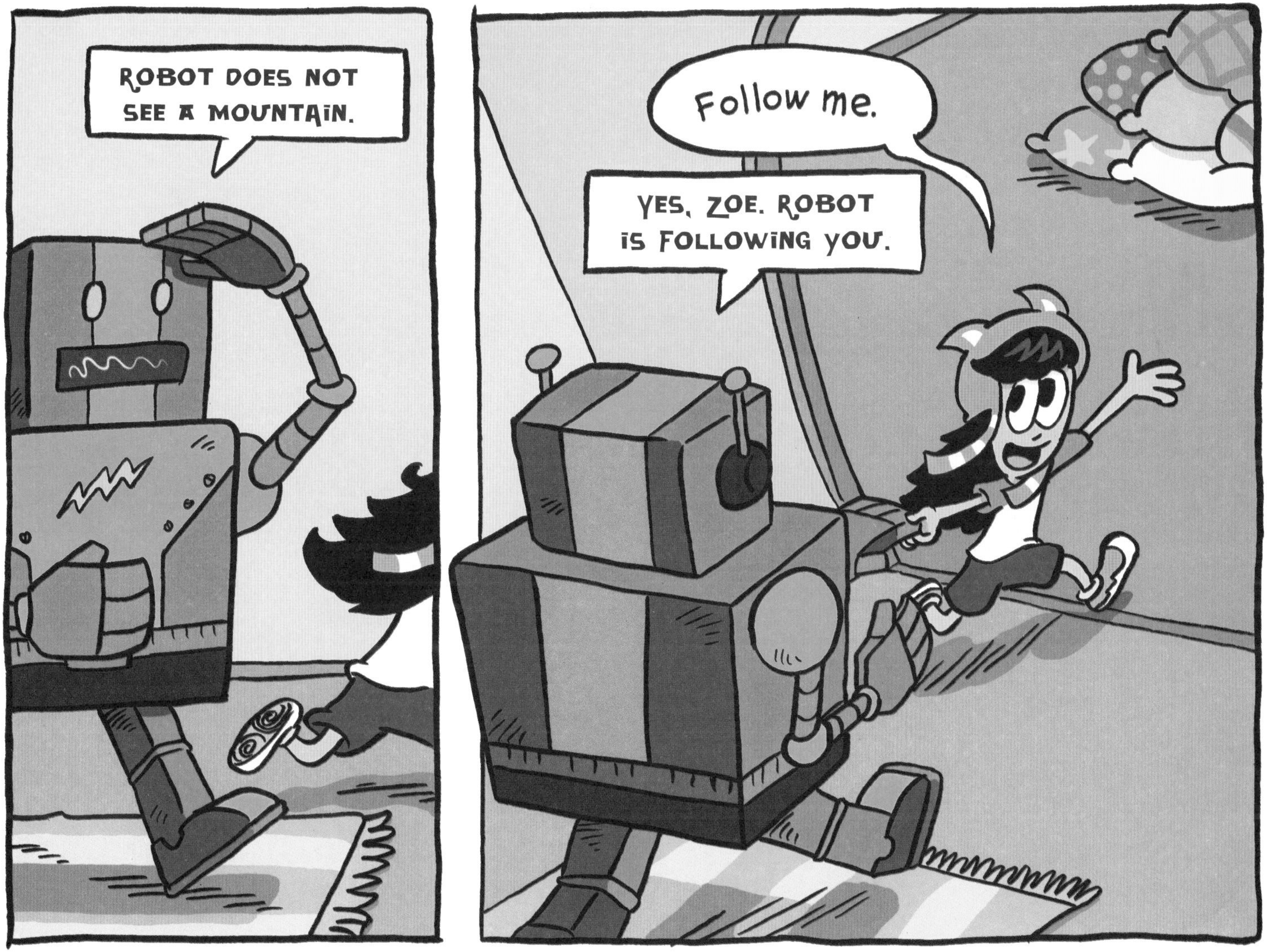
ROBOT DOES NOT SEE A MOUNTAIN.
Follow me.
YES, ZOE. ROBOT IS FOLLOWING YOU.

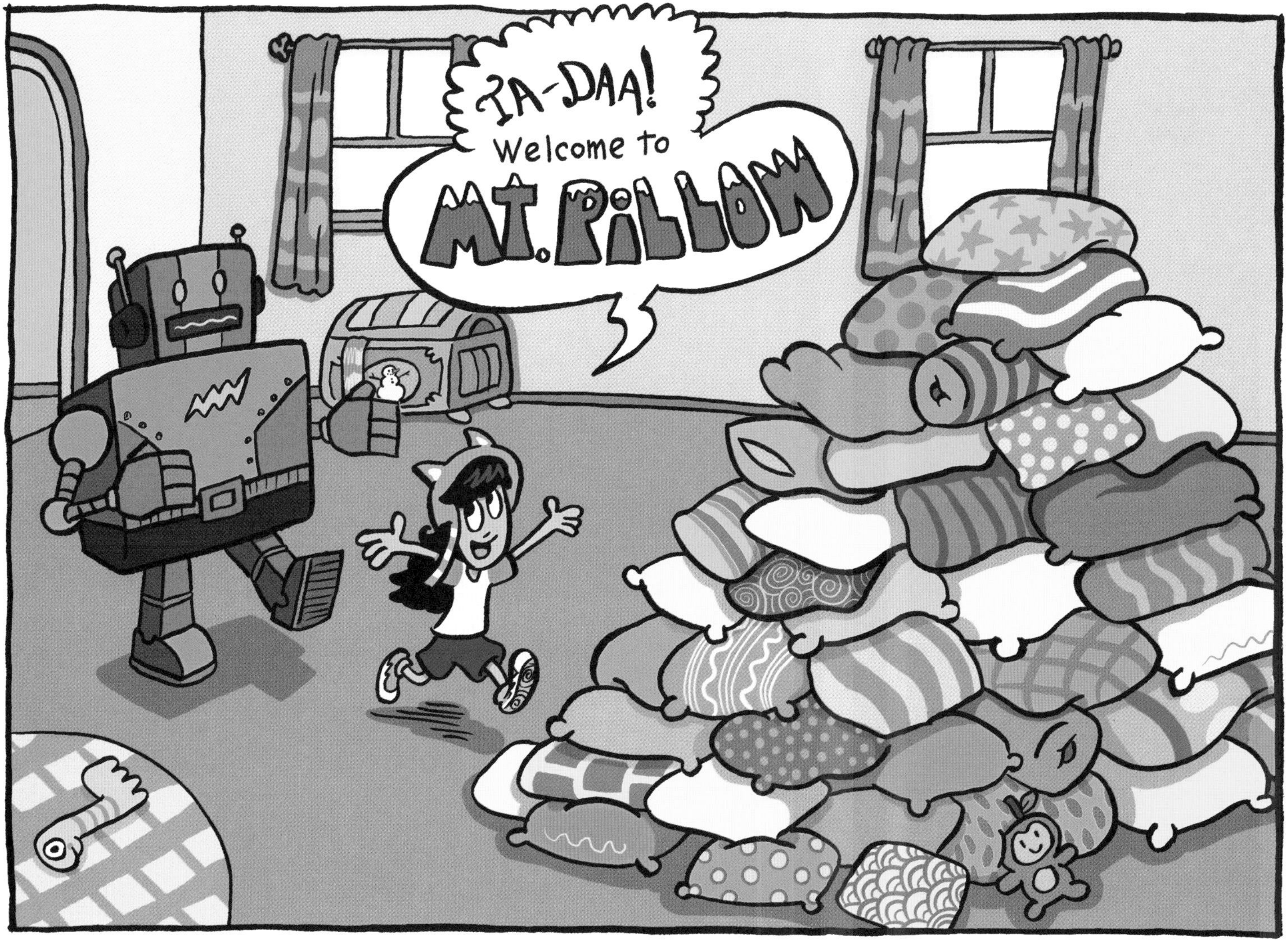
TA-DAA!
Welcome to
MT. PiLLOW

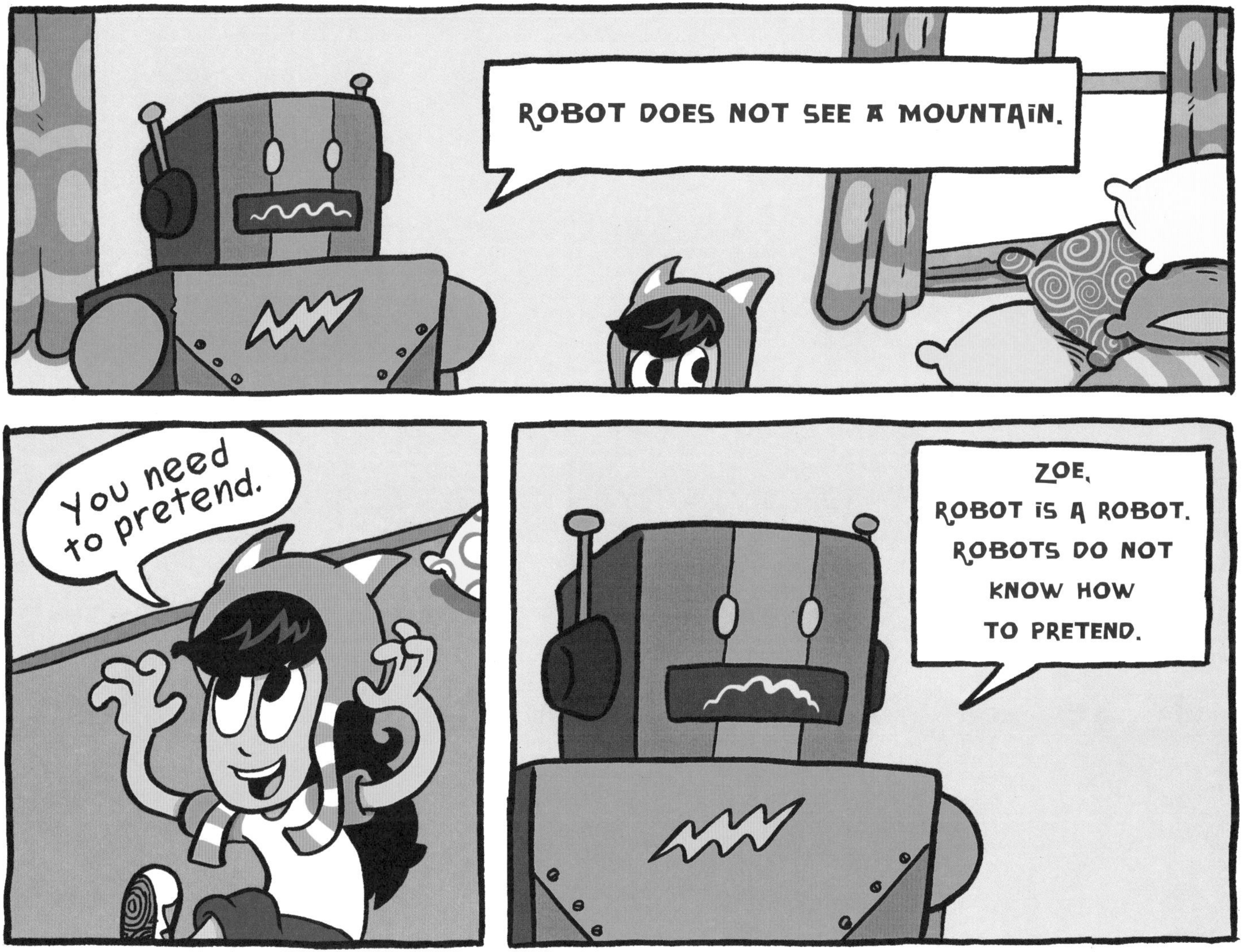
ROBOT DOES NOT SEE A MOUNTAIN.
You need to pretend.
ZOE,
ROBOT IS A ROBOT.
ROBOTS DO NOT
KNOW HOW
TO PRETEND.

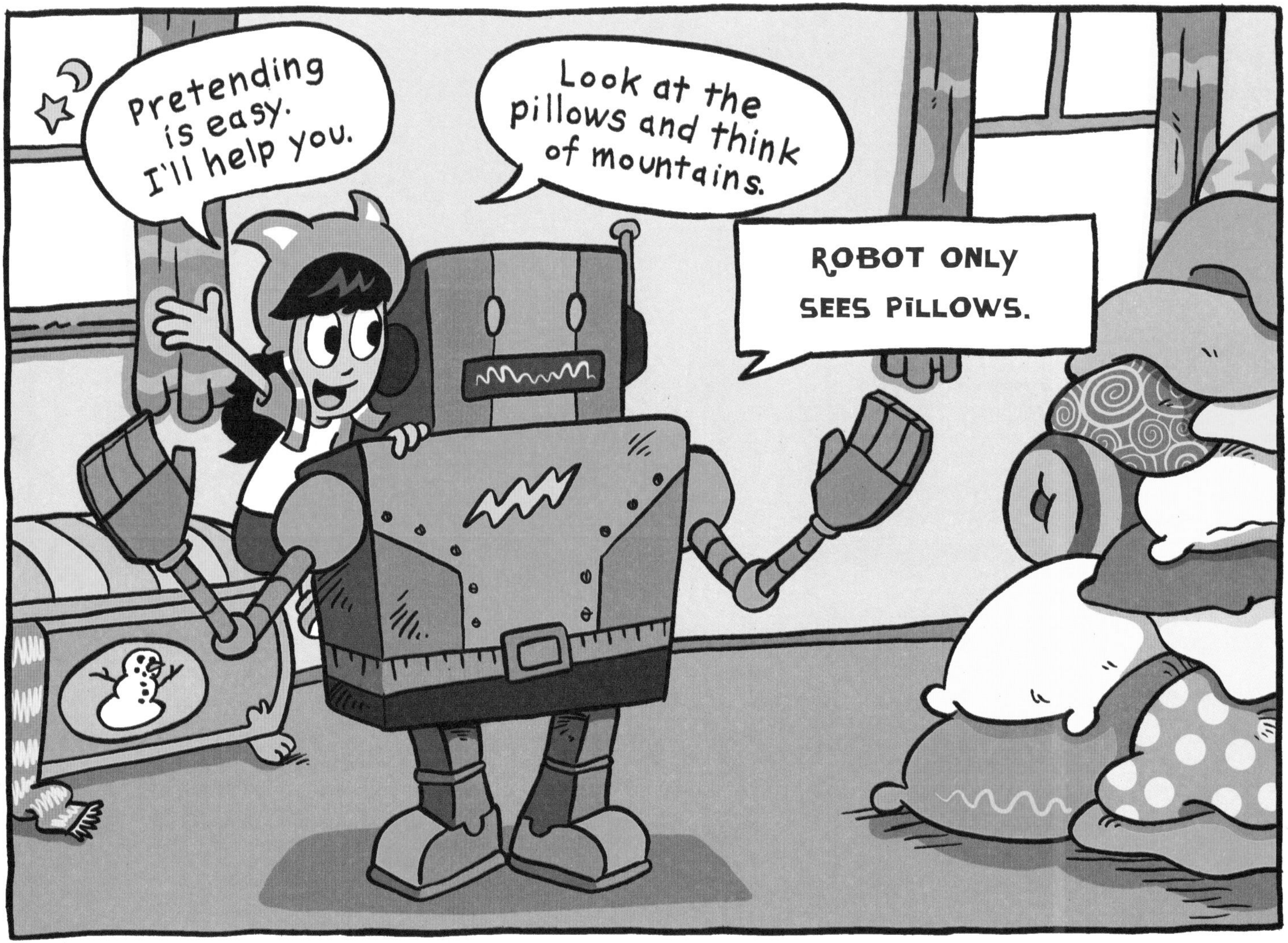
Pretending is easy. I'll help you.
Look at the pillows and think of mountains.
ROBOT ONLY SEES PILLOWS.

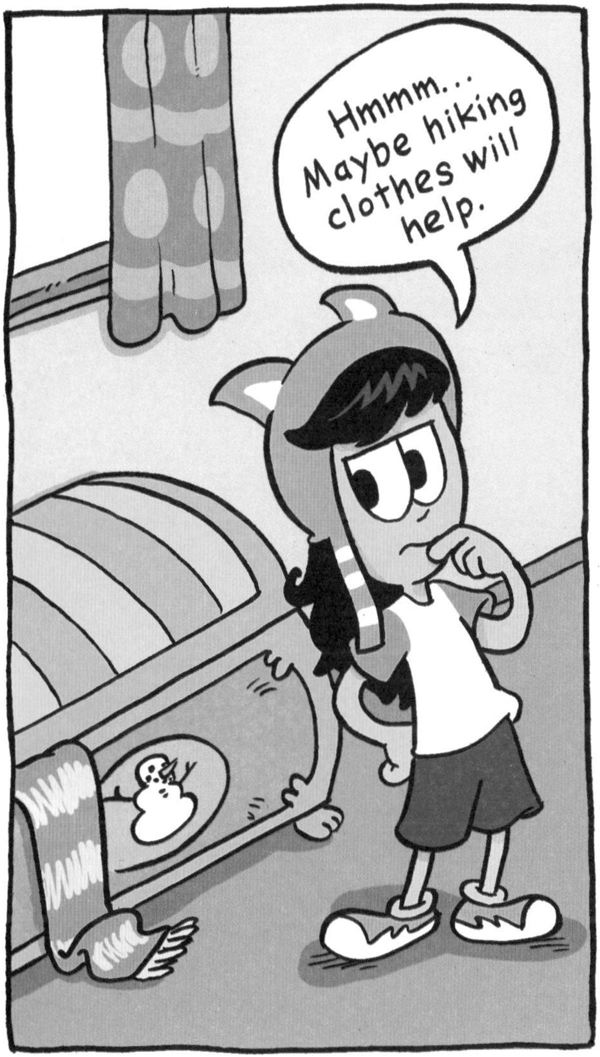
Hmmm... Maybe hiking clothes will help.

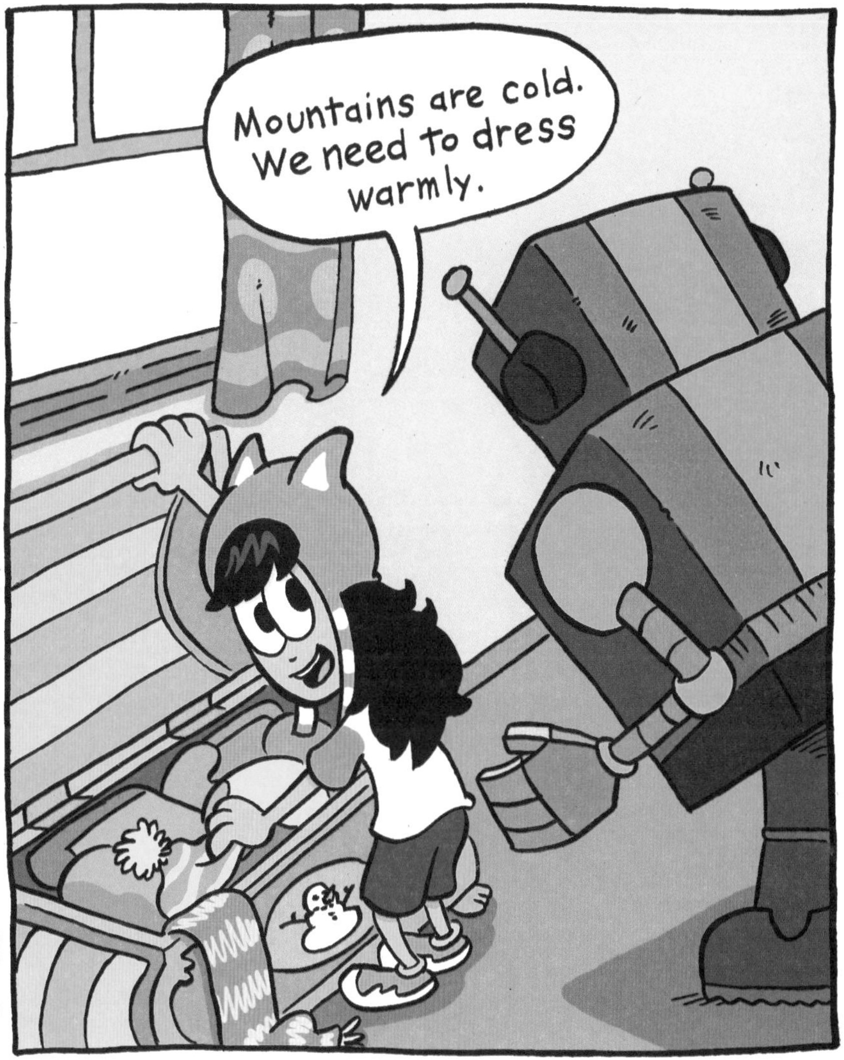
Mountains are cold. We need to dress warmly.

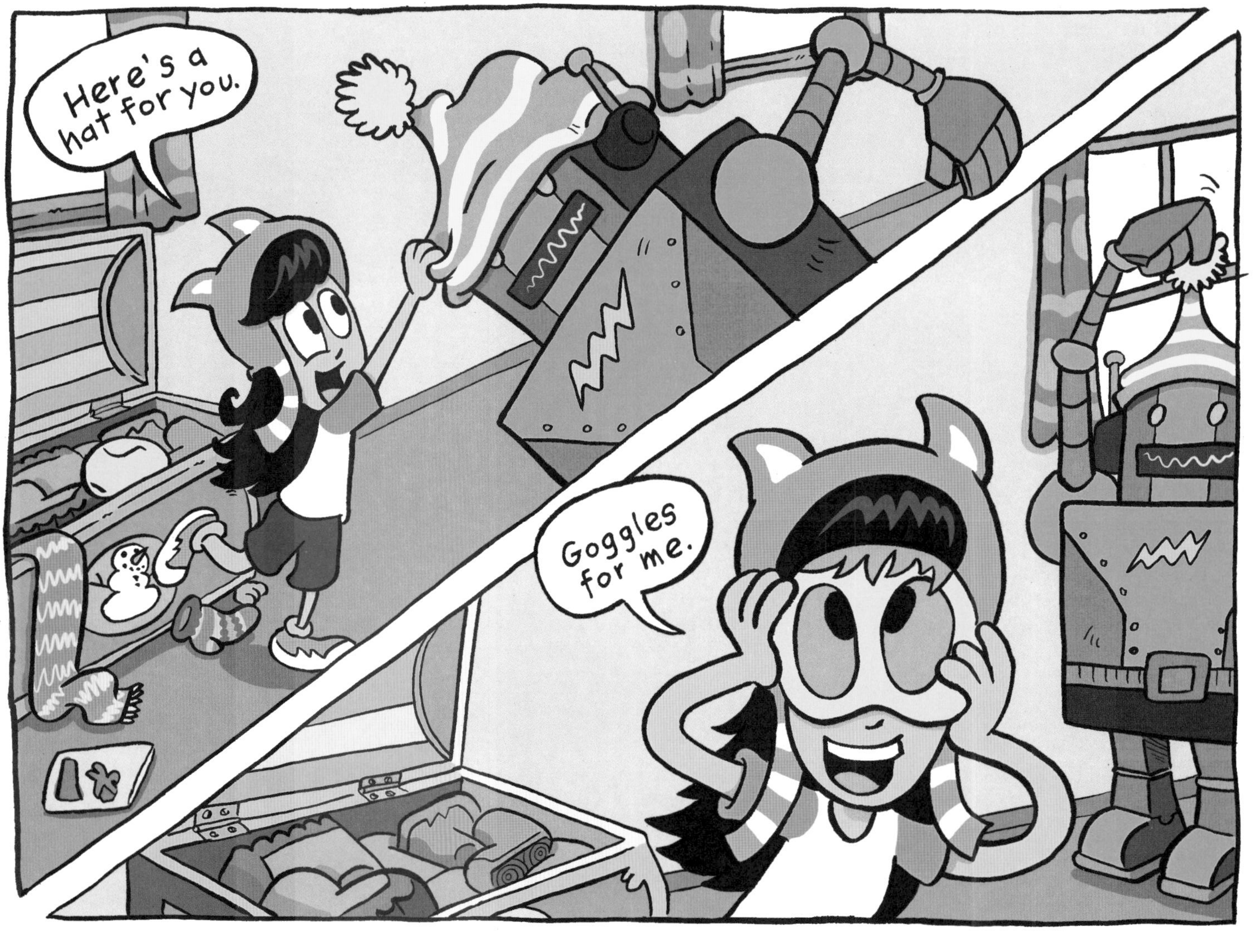
Here's a hat for you.
Goggles for me.

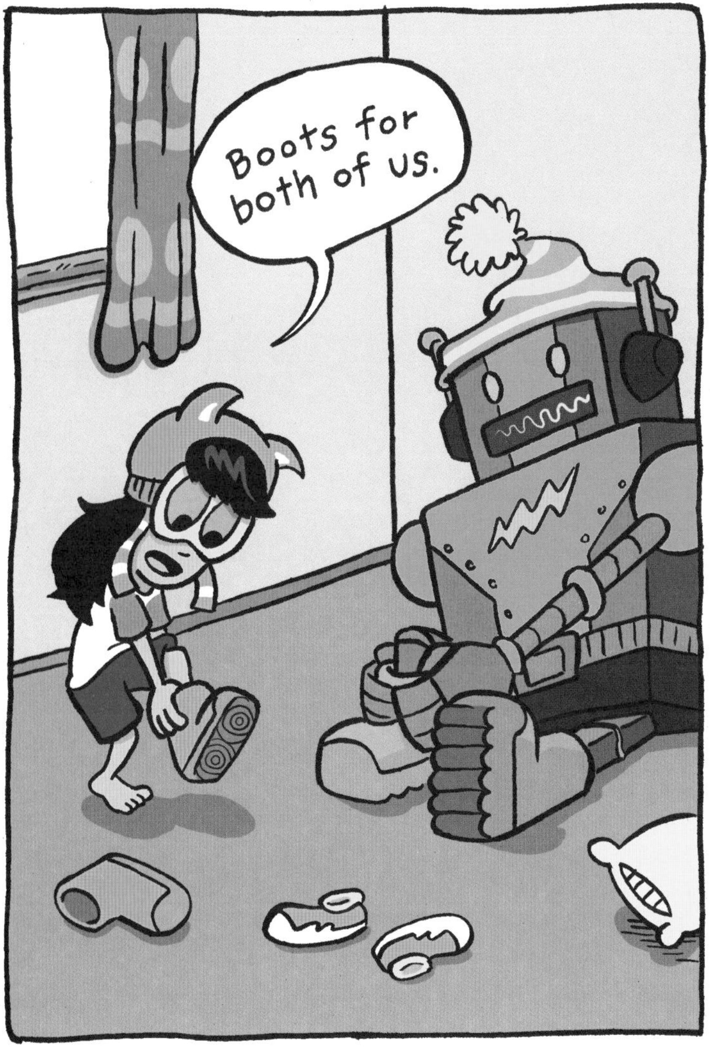
Boots for both of us.
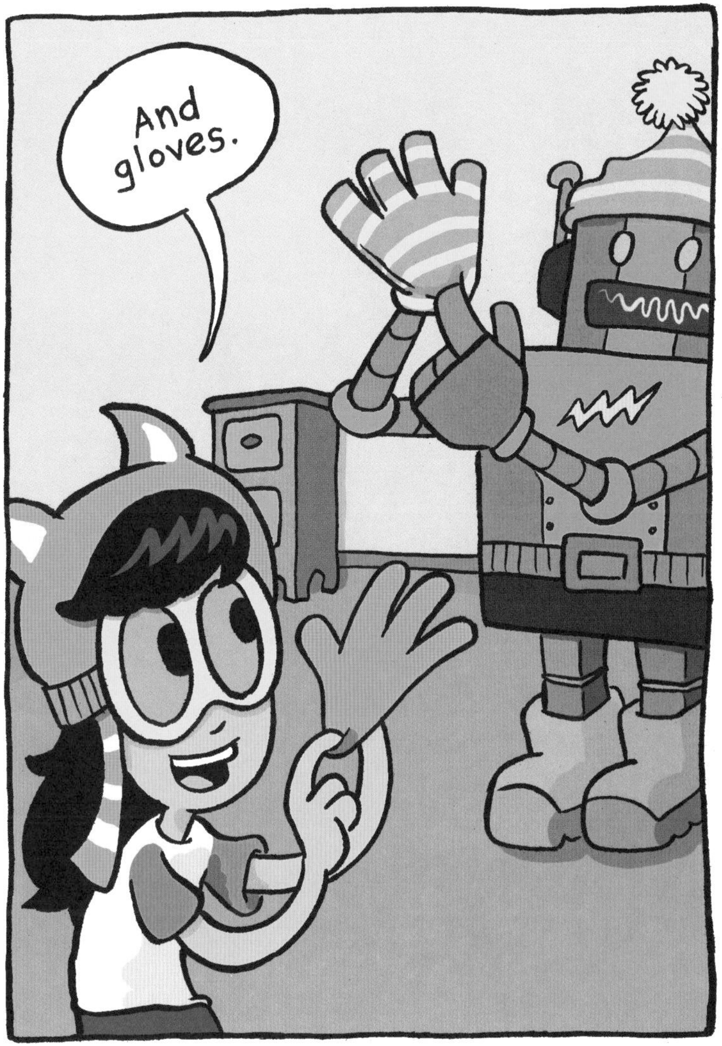
And gloves.

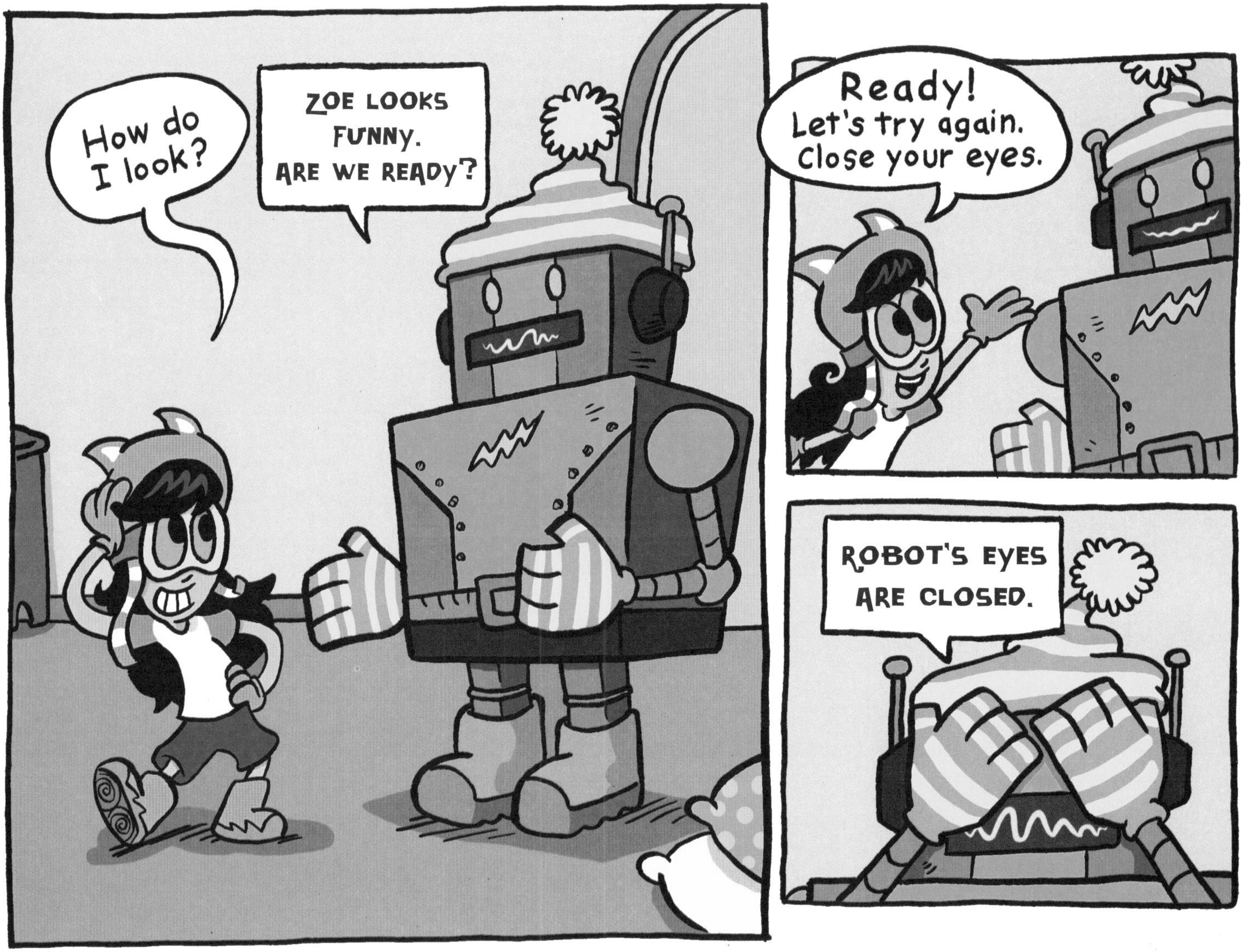
How do I look?
ZOE LOOKS FUNNY. ARE WE READY?
Ready! Let's try again. Close your eyes.
ROBOT'S EYES ARE CLOSED.

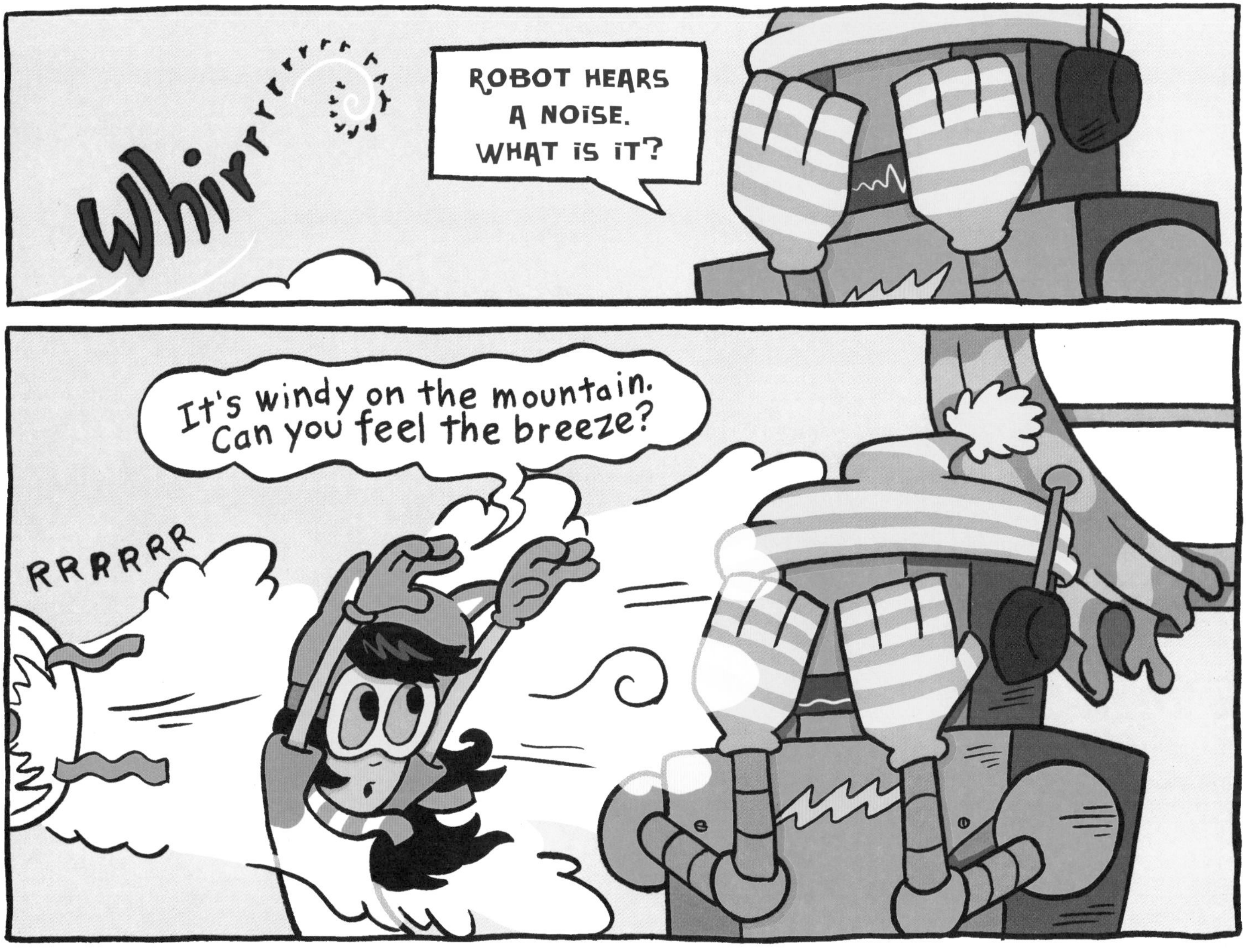
Whirrrrrrrrrrrrrr
ROBOT HEARS A NOISE. WHAT IS IT?
It's windy on the mountain. Can you feel the breeze?
RRRRRR

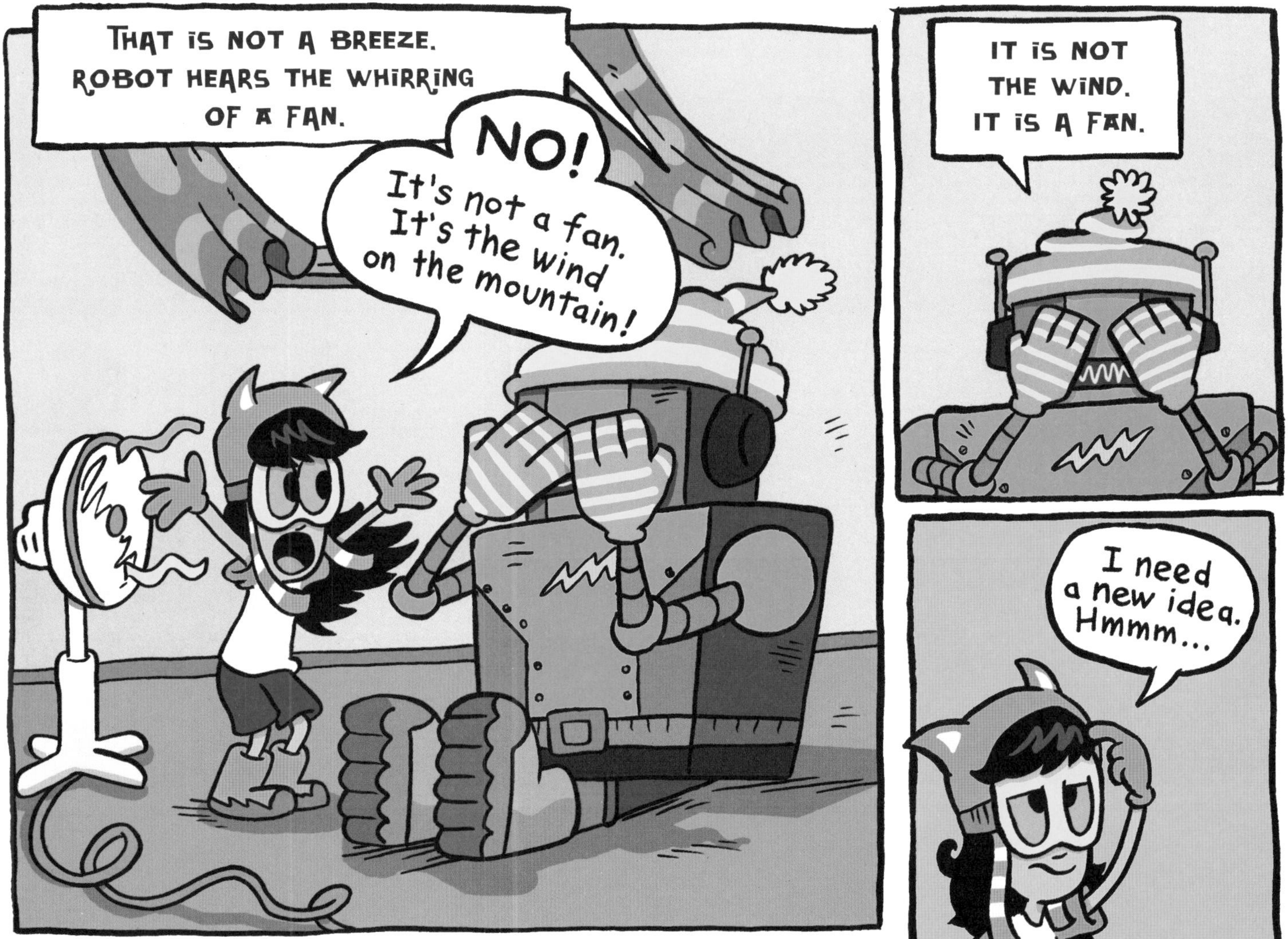
THAT IS NOT A BREEZE. ROBOT HEARS THE WHIRRING OF A FAN.
NO! It's not a fan. It's the wind on the mountain!
IT IS NOT THE WIND. IT IS A FAN.
I need a new idea. Hmmm...

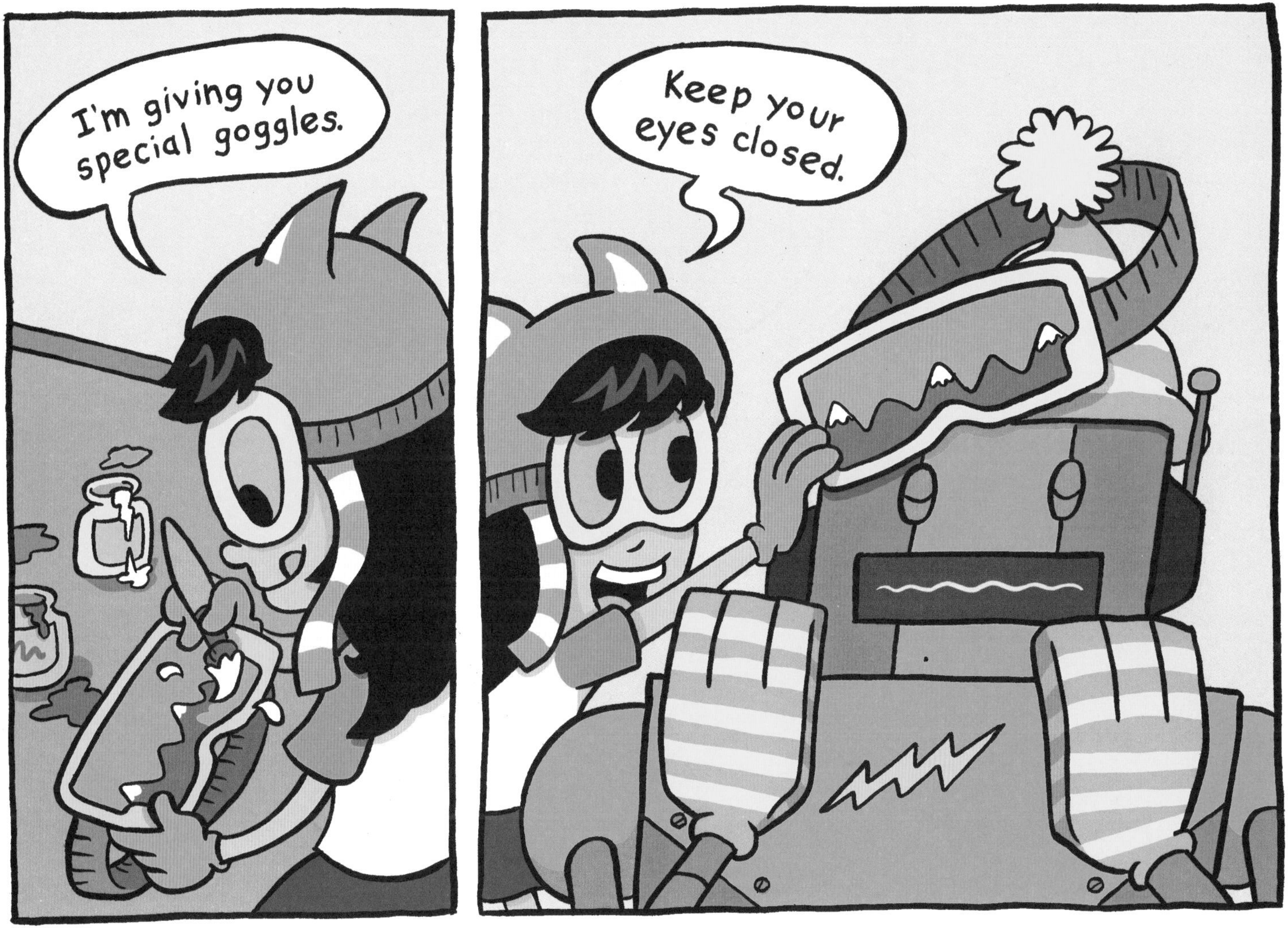
I'm giving you special goggles.
Keep your eyes closed.

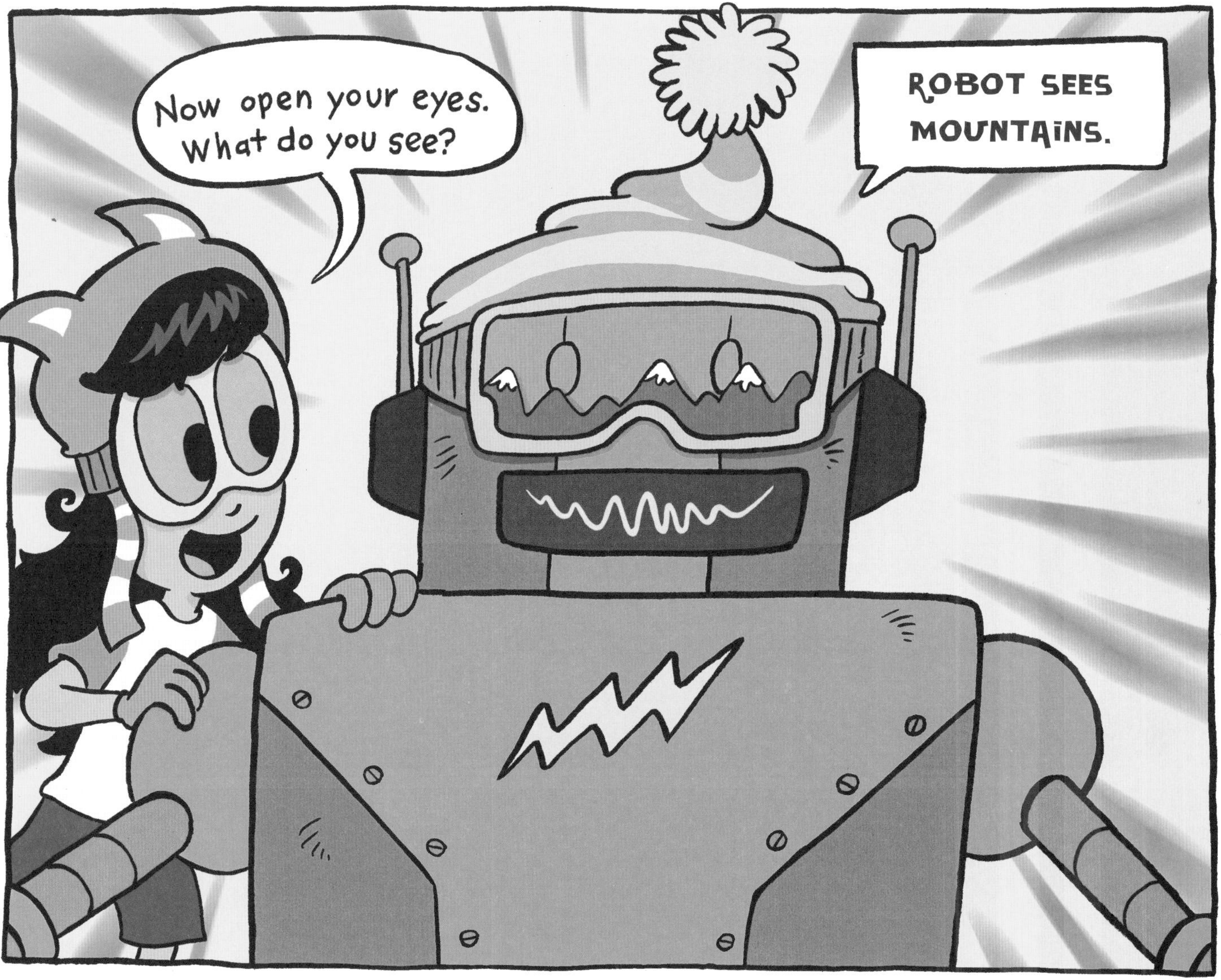
Now open your eyes. What do you see?
ROBOT SEES MOUNTAINS.

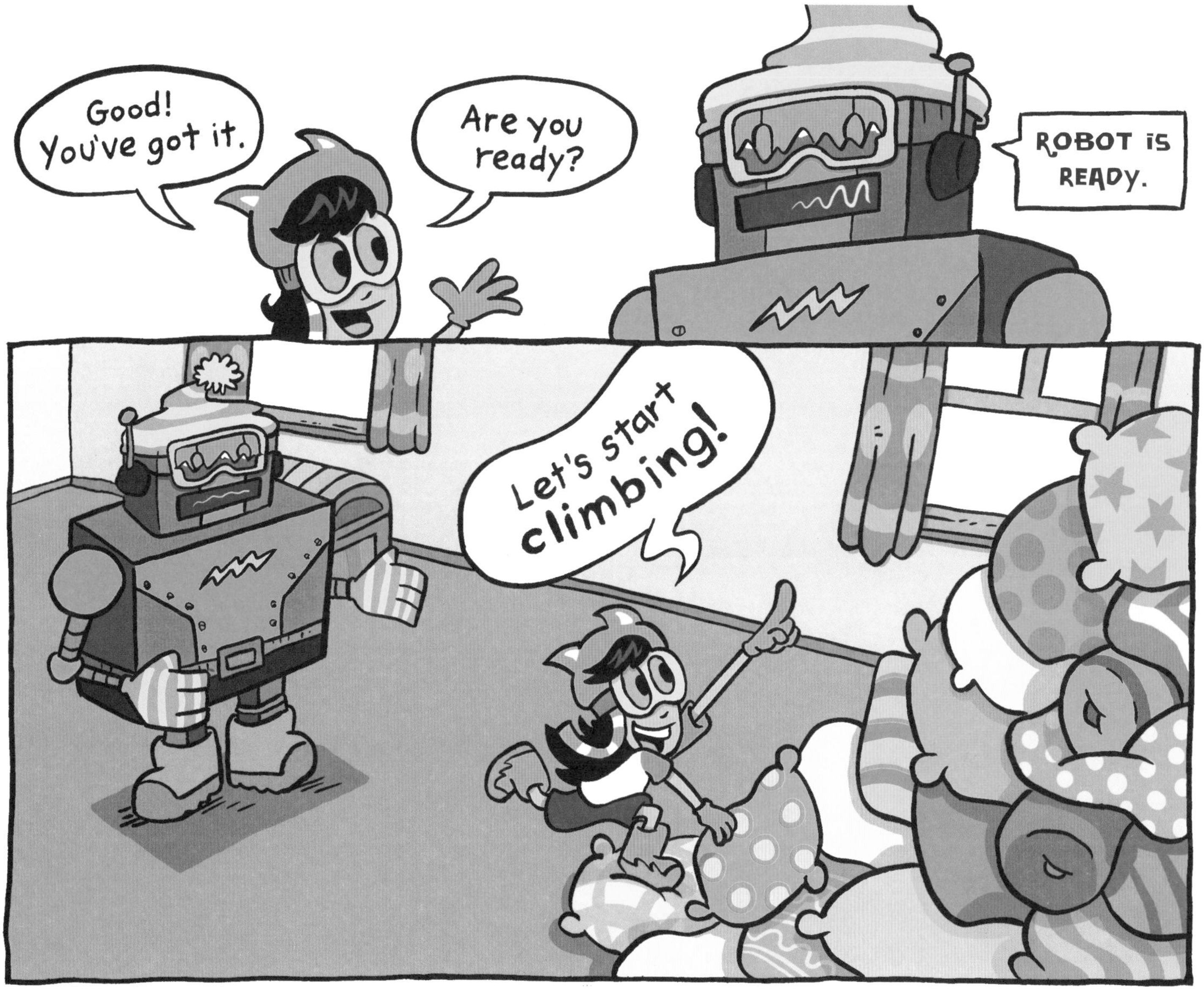
Good! You've got it.
Are you ready?
ROBOT IS READY.
Let's start climbing!

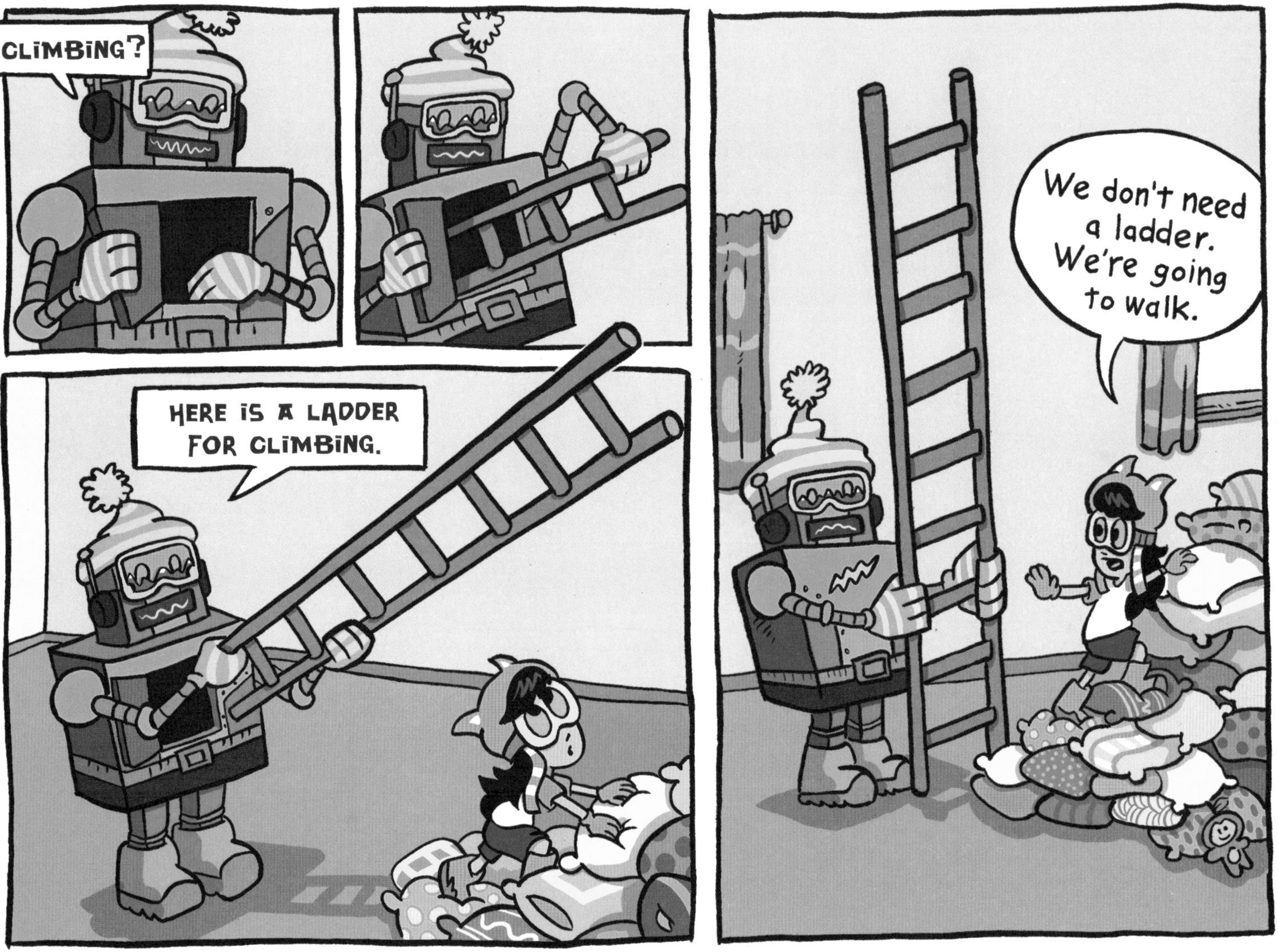
CLIMBING?
HERE IS A LADDER FOR CLIMBING.
We don't need a ladder. We're going to walk.

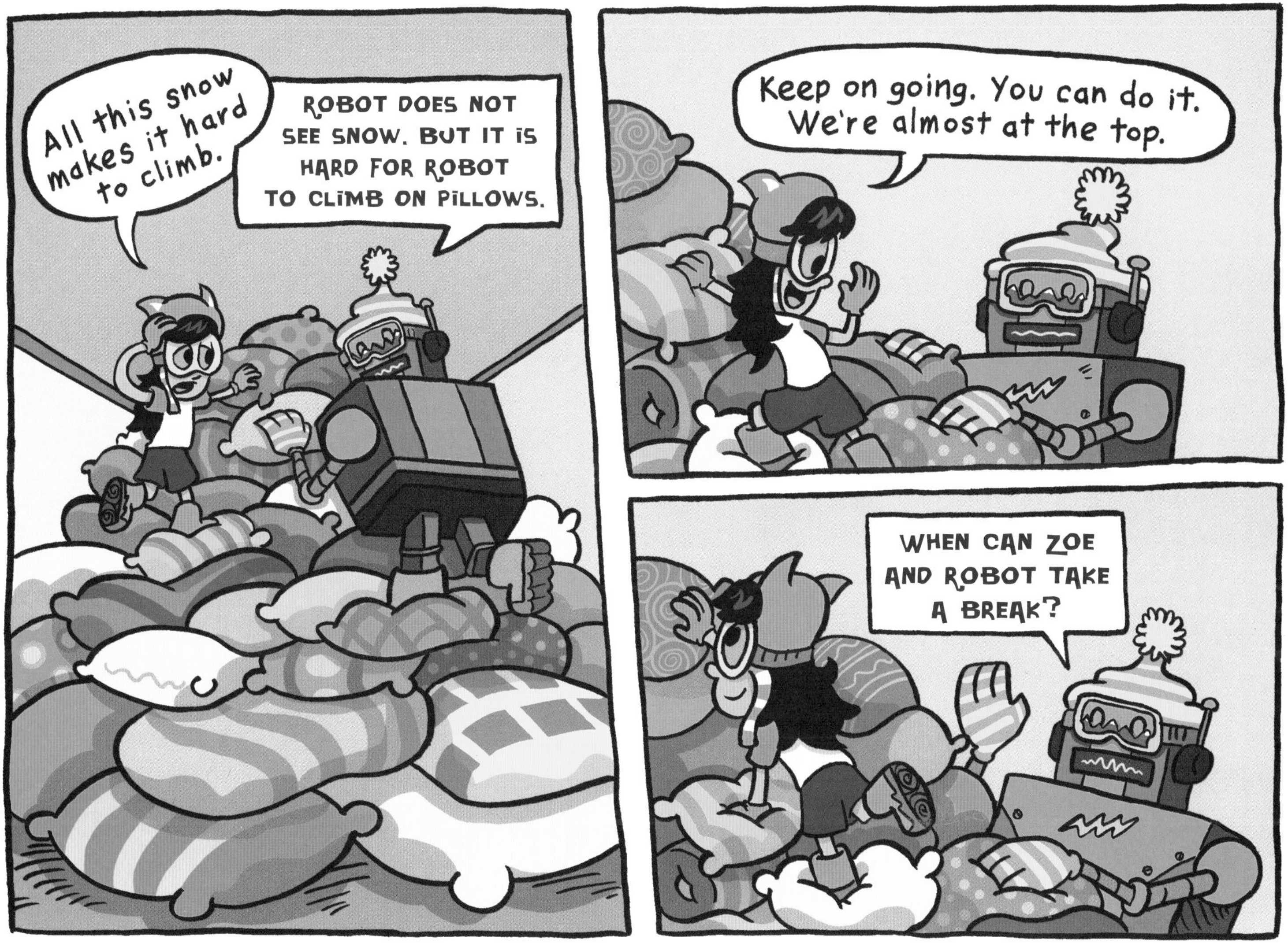
All this snow makes it hard to climb.
ROBOT DOES NOT SEE SNOW. BUT IT IS HARD FOR ROBOT TO CLIMB ON PILLOWS.
Keep on going. You can do it. We're almost at the top.
WHEN CAN ZOE AND ROBOT TAKE A BREAK?

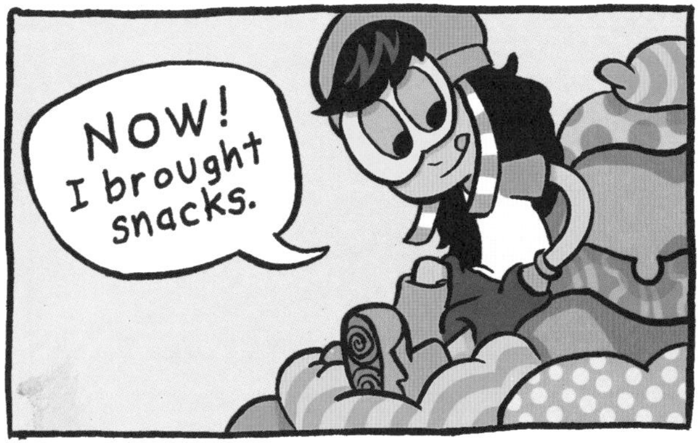
NOW! I brought snacks.

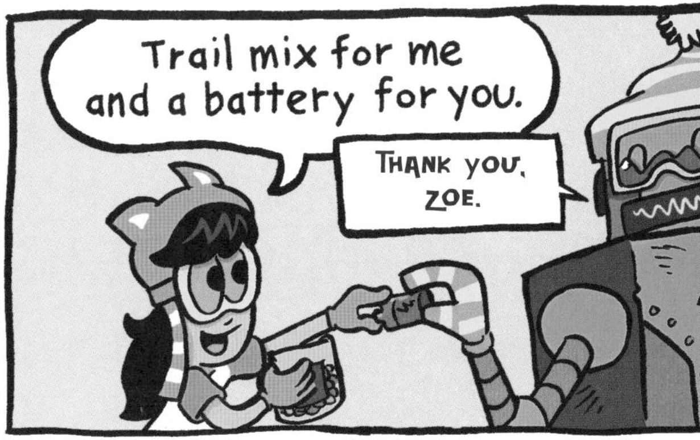
Trail mix for me and a battery for you.
THANK YOU, ZOE.

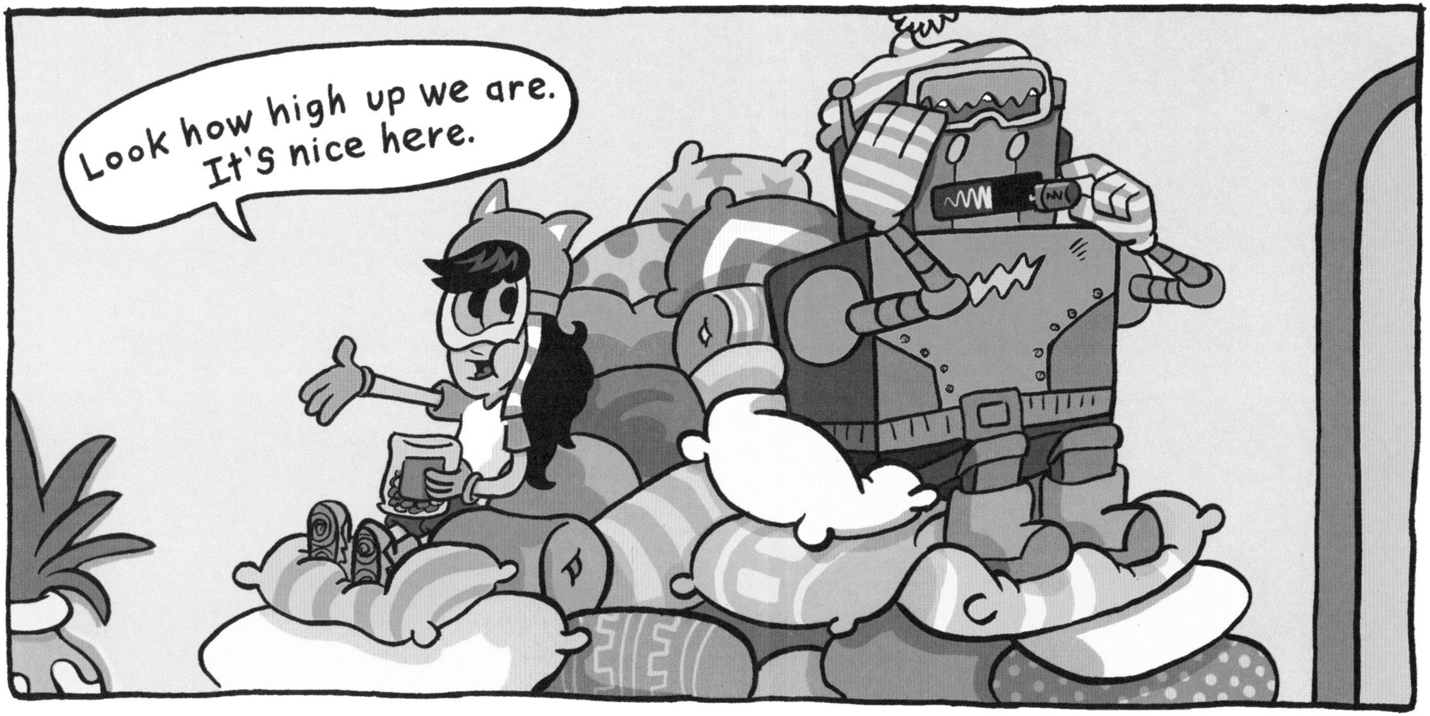
Look how high up we are. It's nice here.

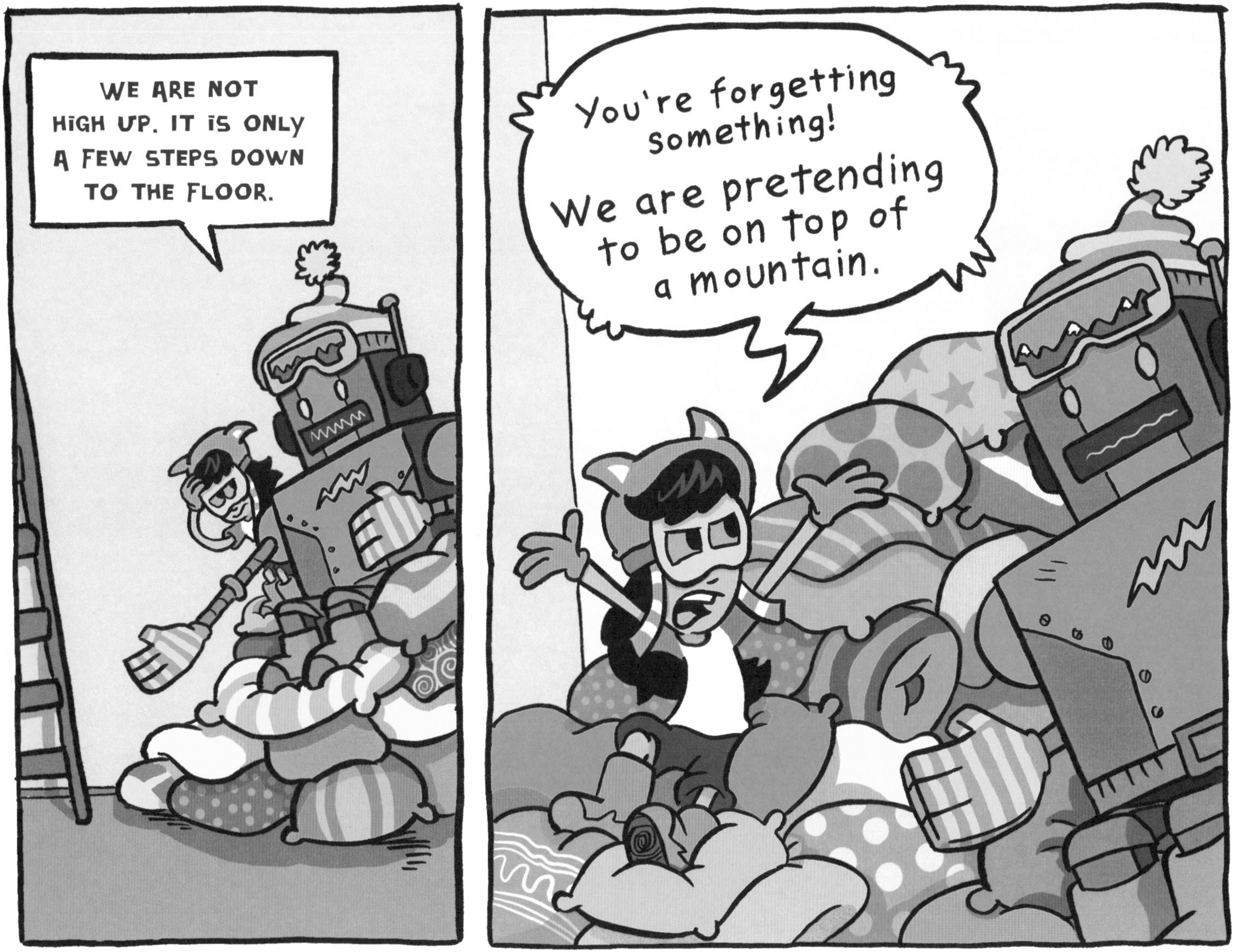
WE ARE NOT HIGH UP. IT IS ONLY A FEW STEPS DOWN TO THE FLOOR.
You're forgetting something!
We are pretending to be on top of a mountain.

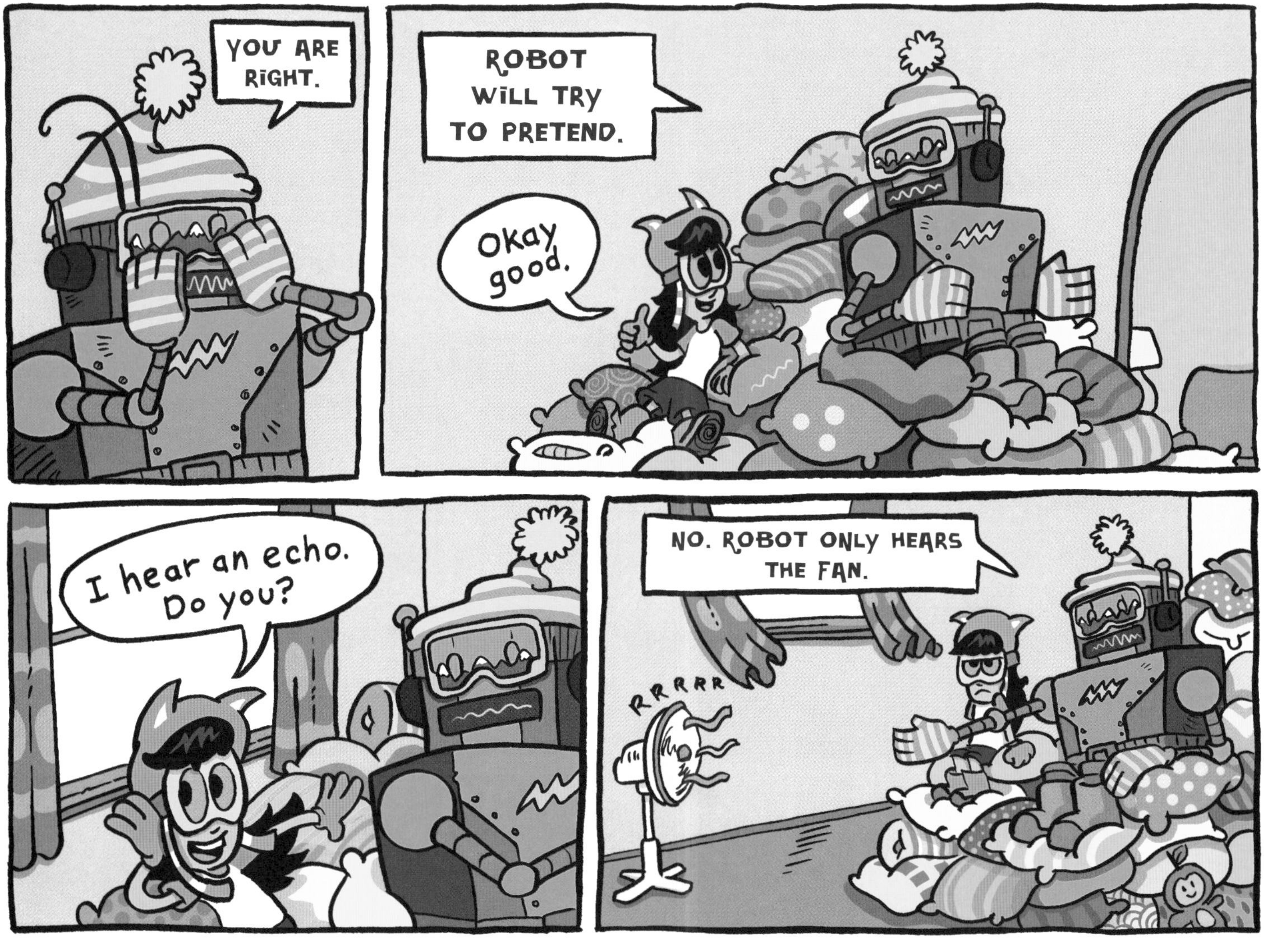
YOU ARE RIGHT.
ROBOT WILL TRY TO PRETEND.
Okay good.
I hear an echo. Do you?
NO. ROBOT ONLY HEARS THE FAN.
RRRRR

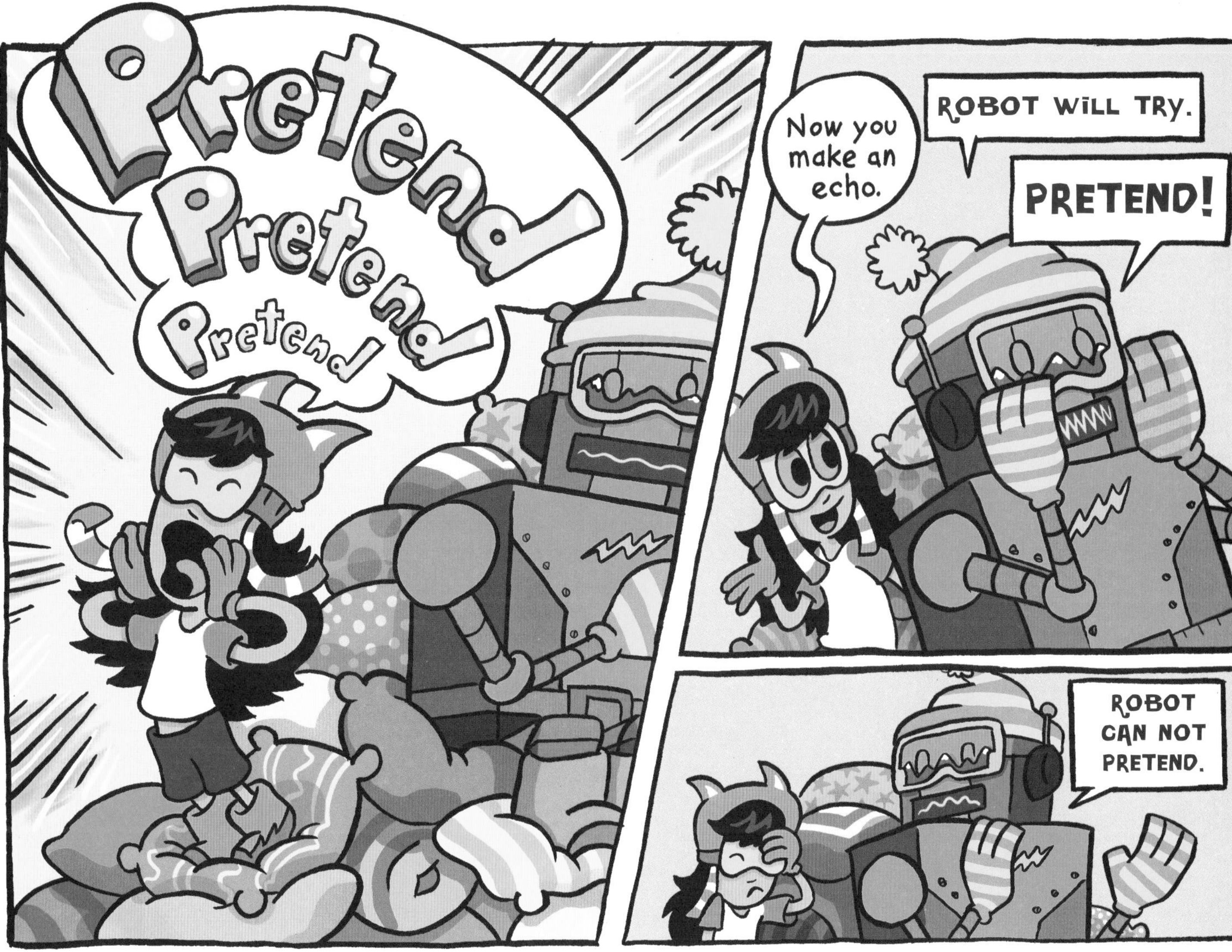

Pretend
Pretend
Pretend
Now you make an echo.
ROBOT WILL TRY.
PRETEND!
ROBOT CAN NOT PRETEND.

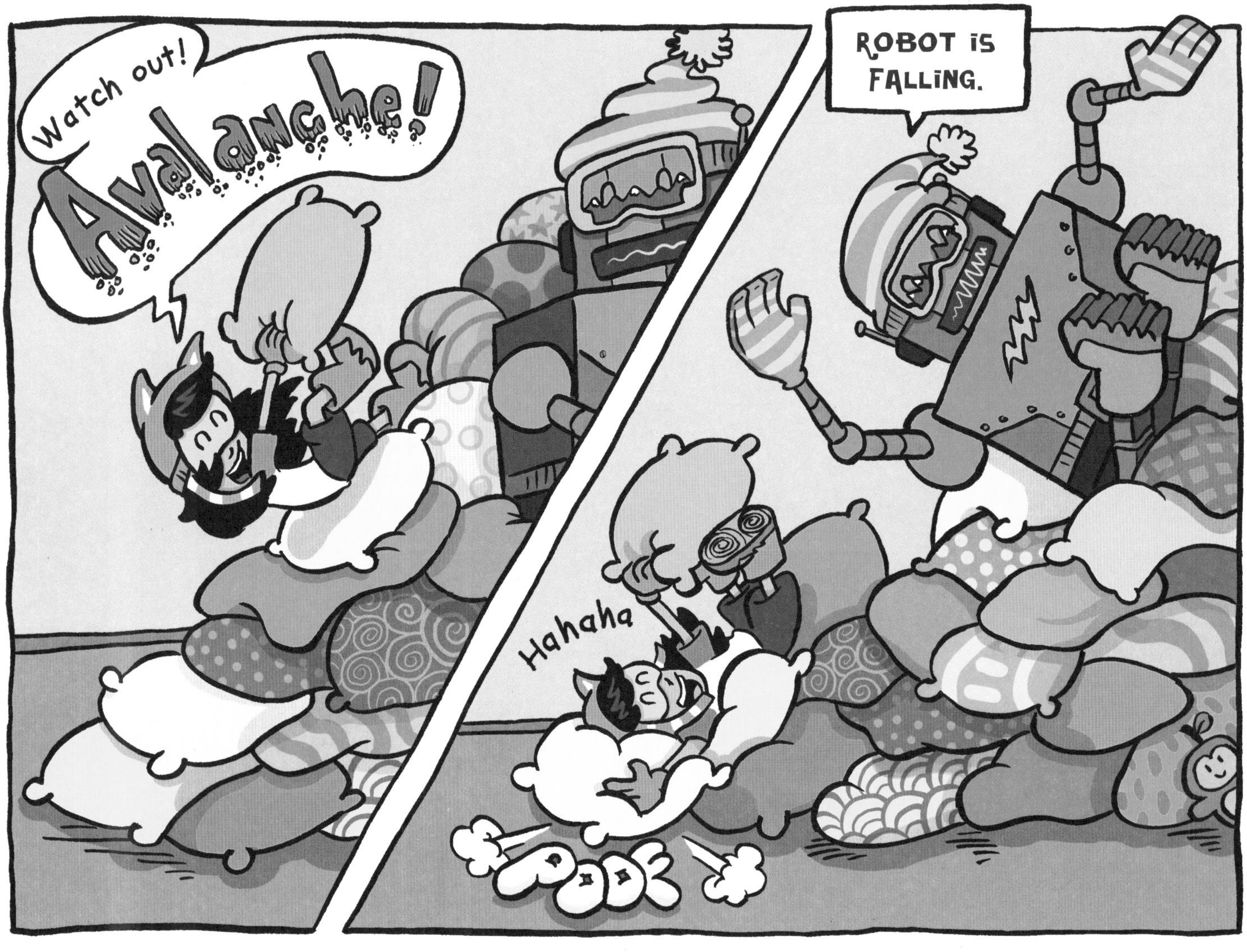
Watch out! Avalanche!
ROBOT IS FALLING.
Hahaha
POOF

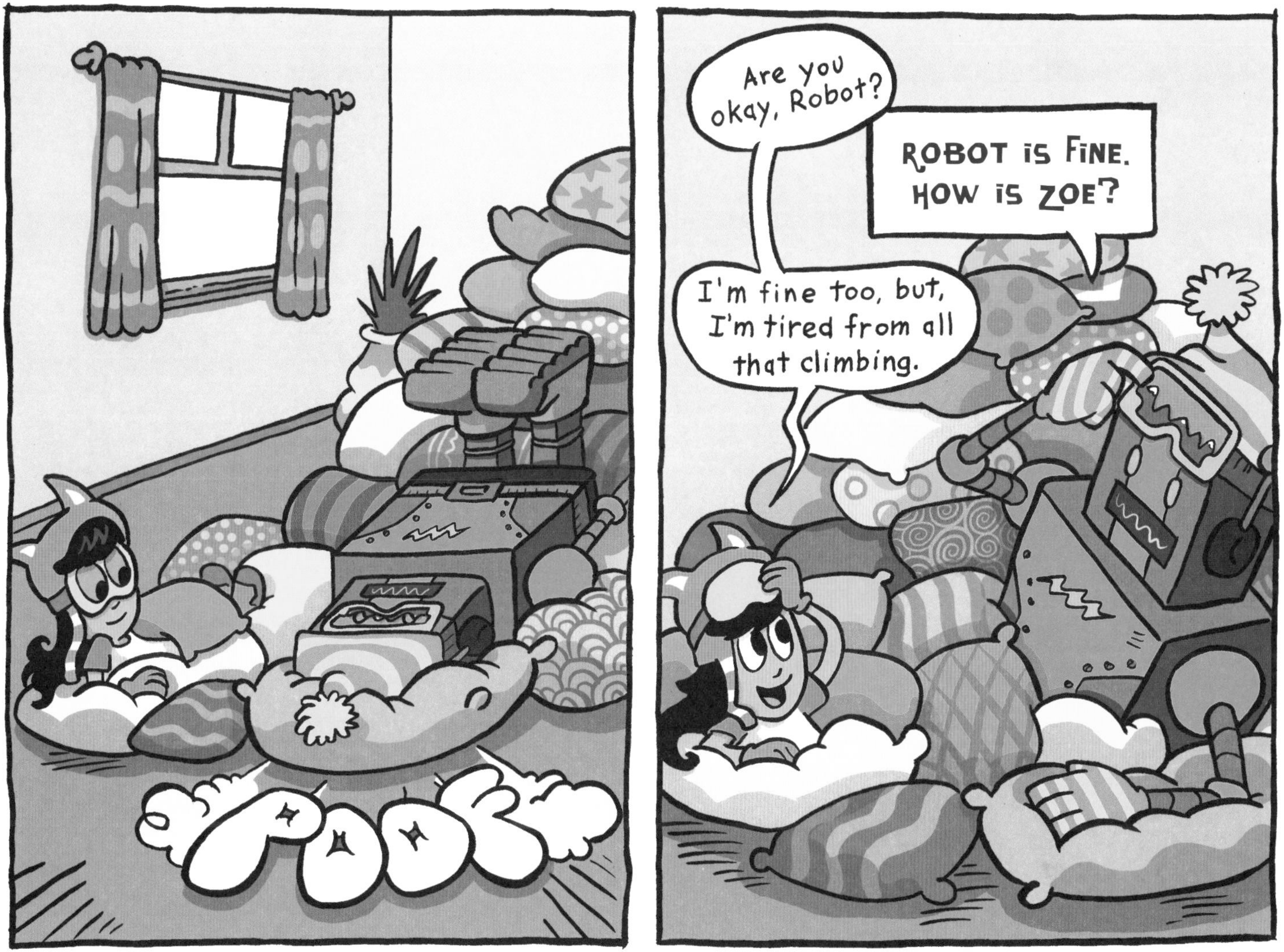
Are you okay, Robot?
ROBOT IS FINE. HOW IS ZOE?
I'm fine too, but, I'm tired from all that climbing.

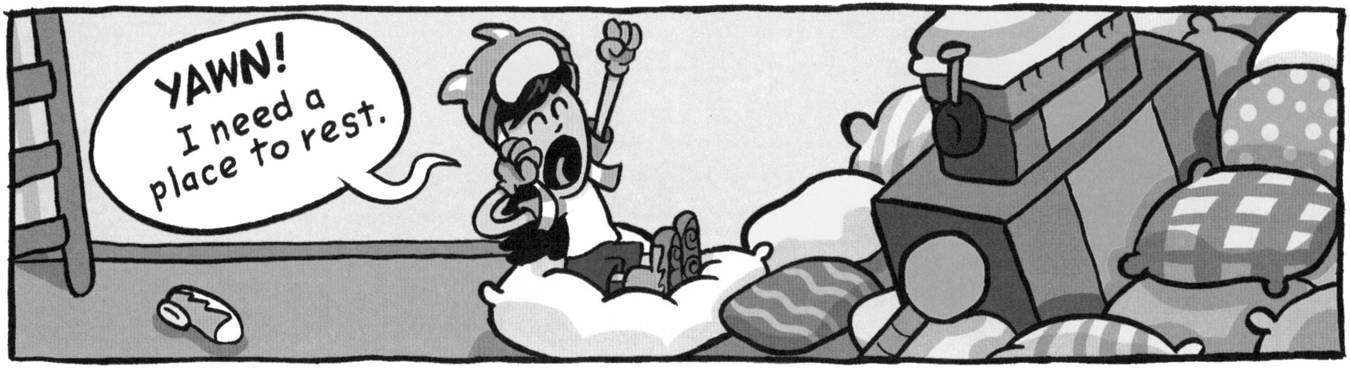
YAWN! I need a place to rest.

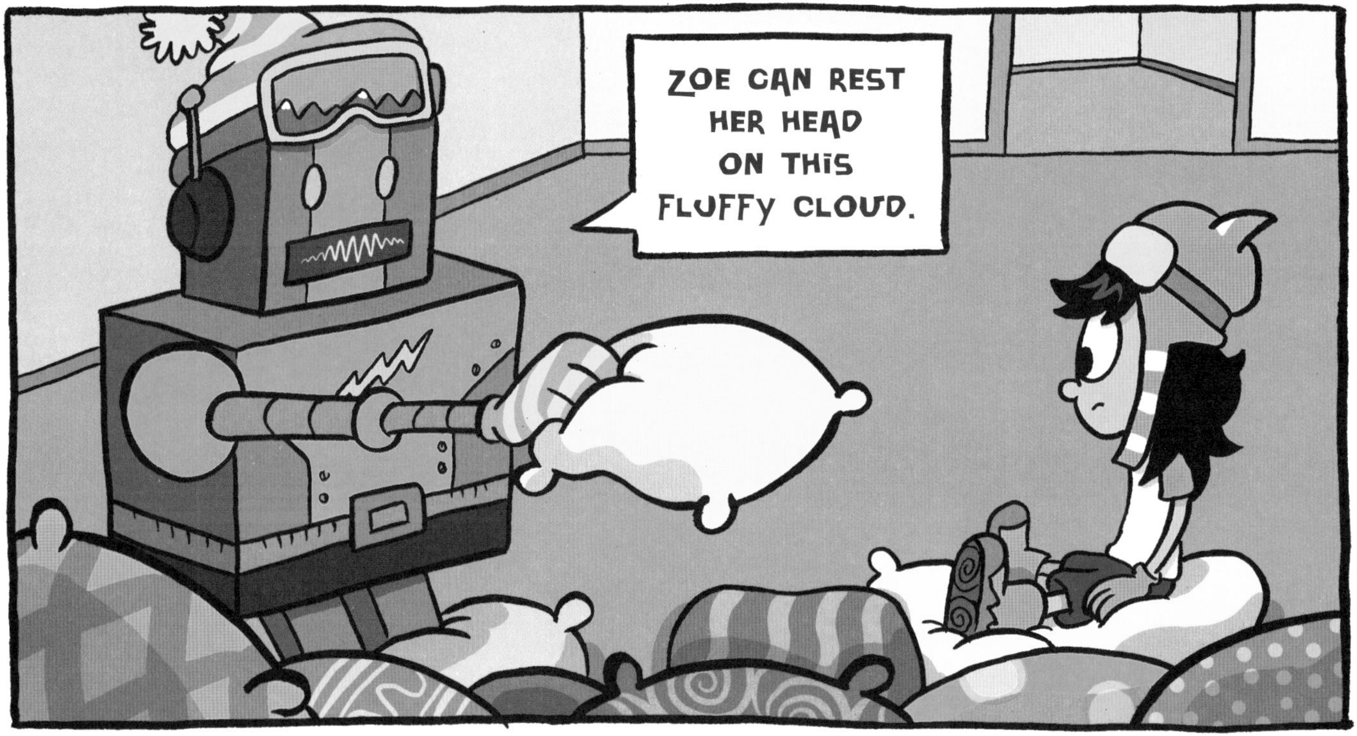
ZOE CAN REST HER HEAD ON THIS FLUFFY CLOUD.

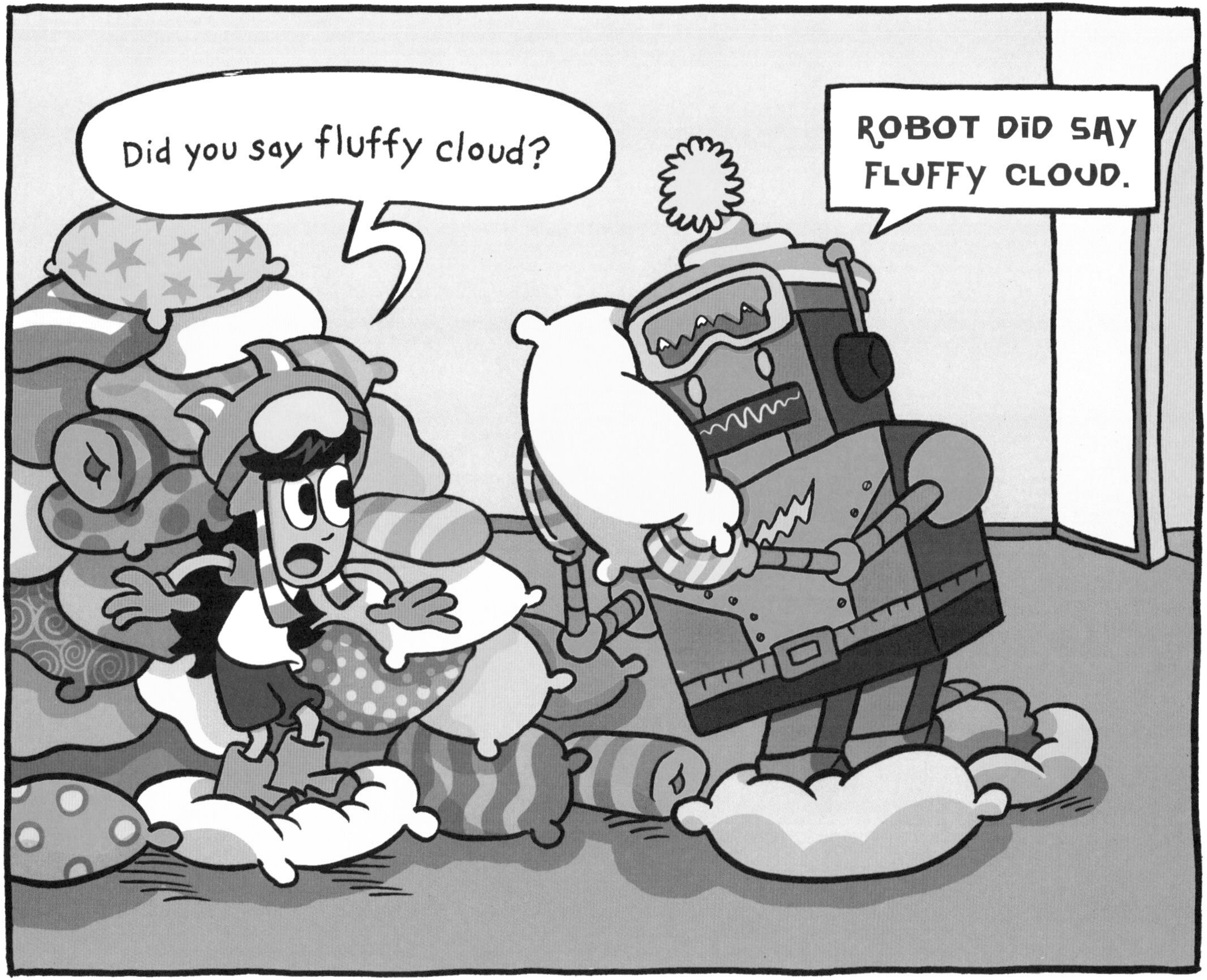
Did you say fluffy cloud?
ROBOT DID SAY FLUFFY CLOUD.

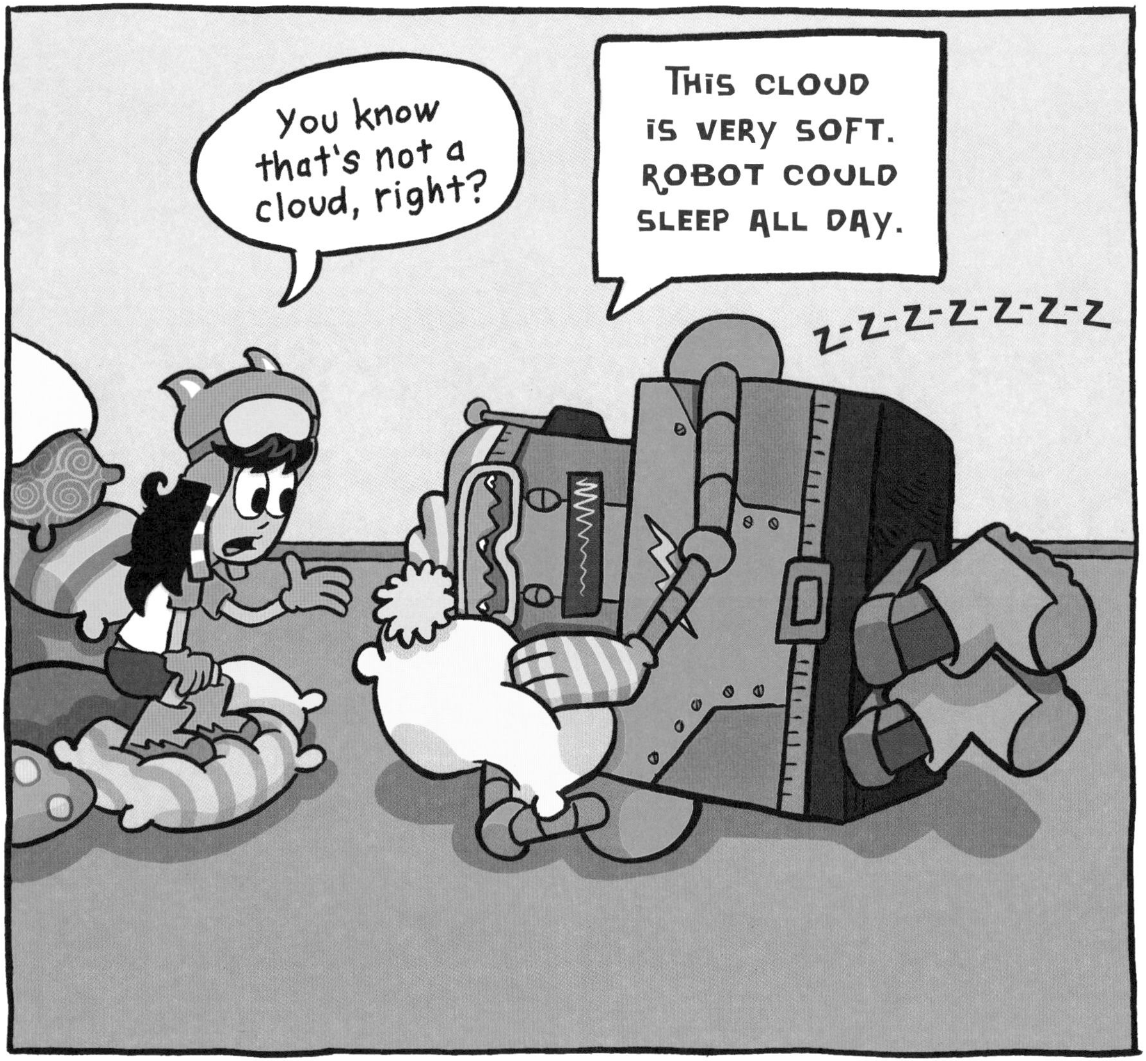
You know that's not a cloud, right?
THIS CLOUD IS VERY SOFT. ROBOT COULD SLEEP ALL DAY.
Z-Z-Z-Z-Z-Z-Z

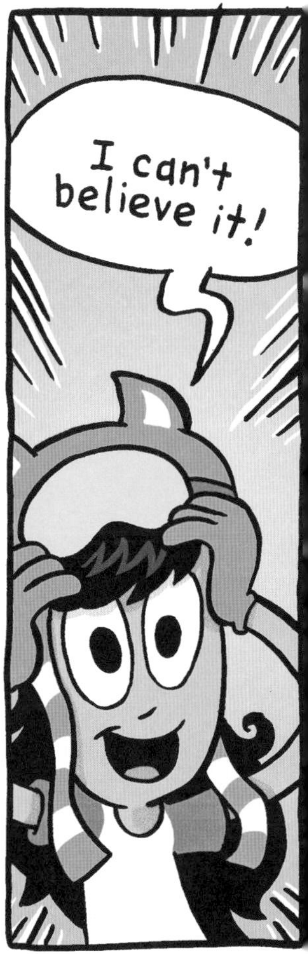
I can't believe it!

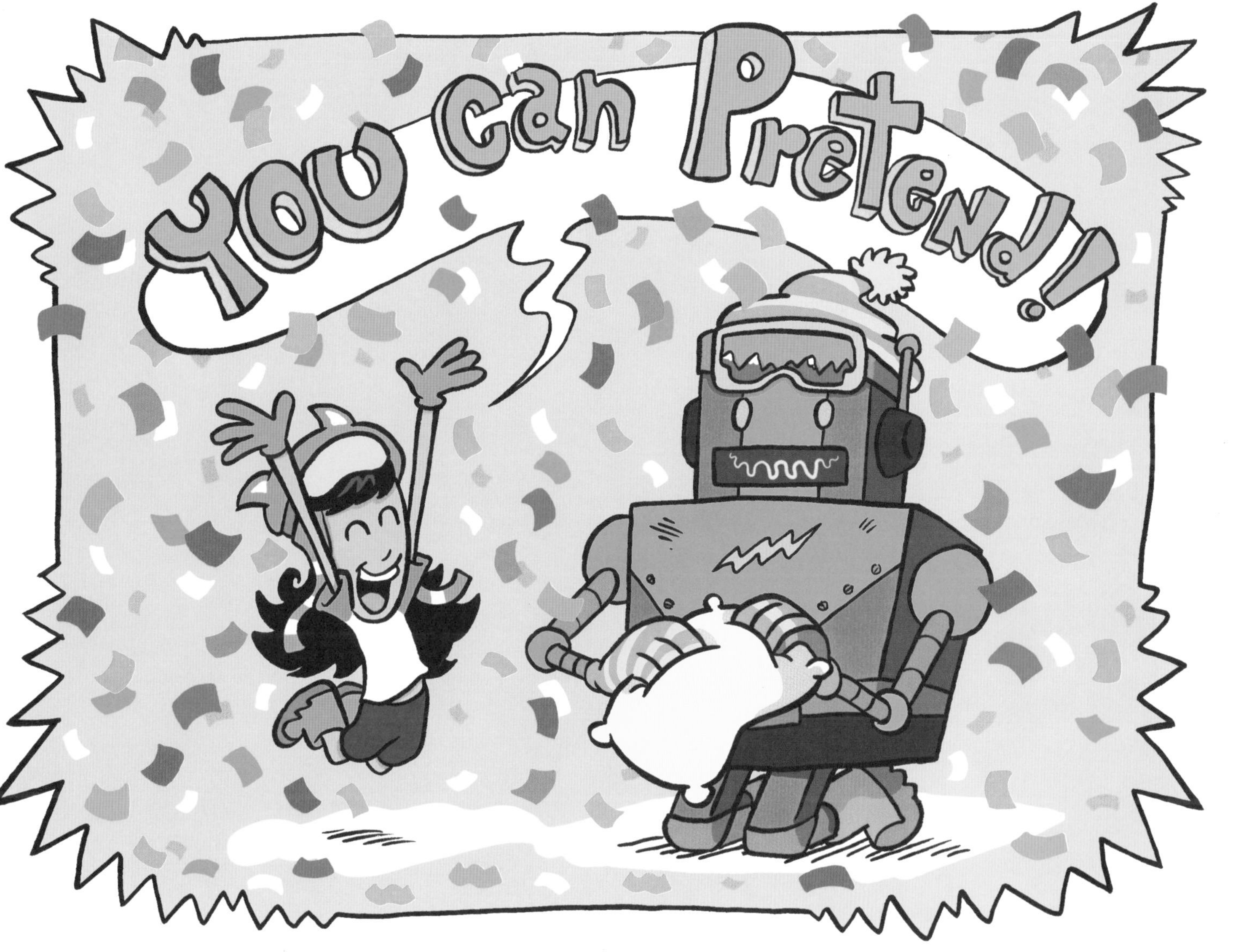
YOU can Pretend!!

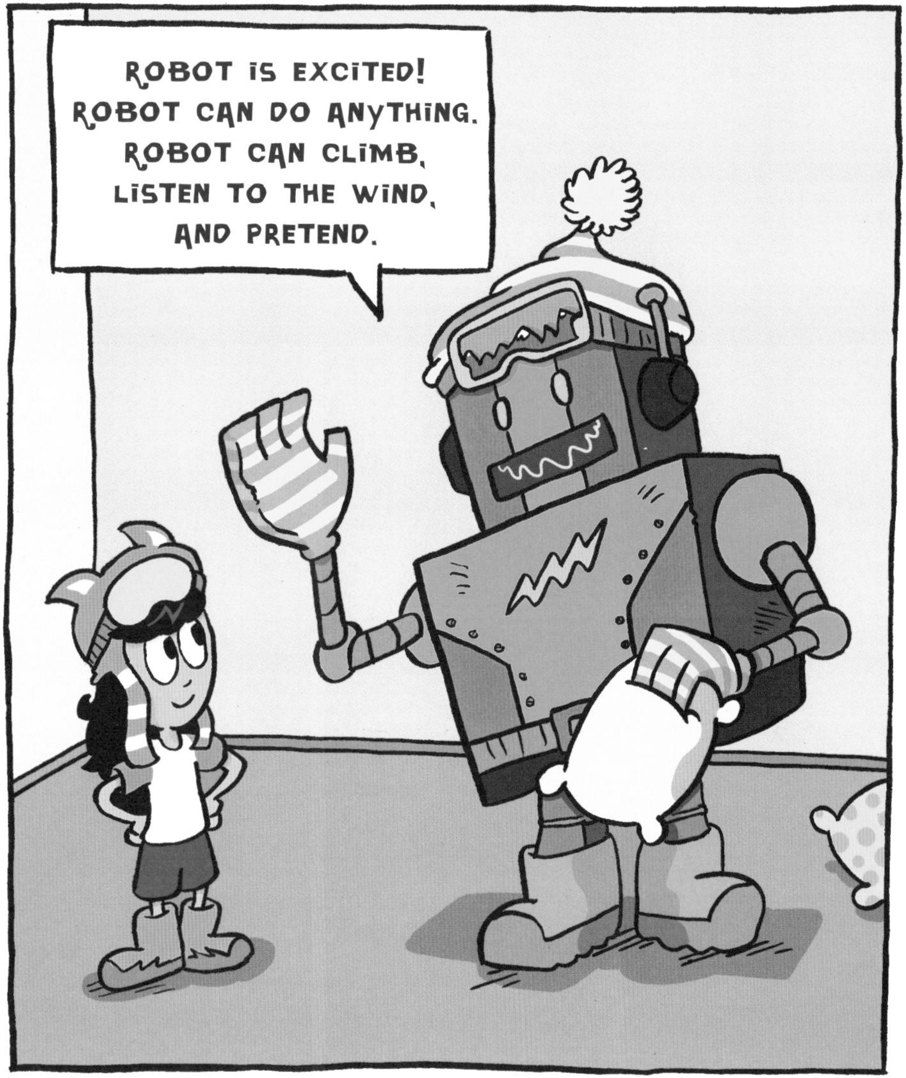
ROBOT IS EXCITED! ROBOT CAN DO ANYTHING. ROBOT CAN CLIMB, LISTEN TO THE WIND, AND PRETEND.

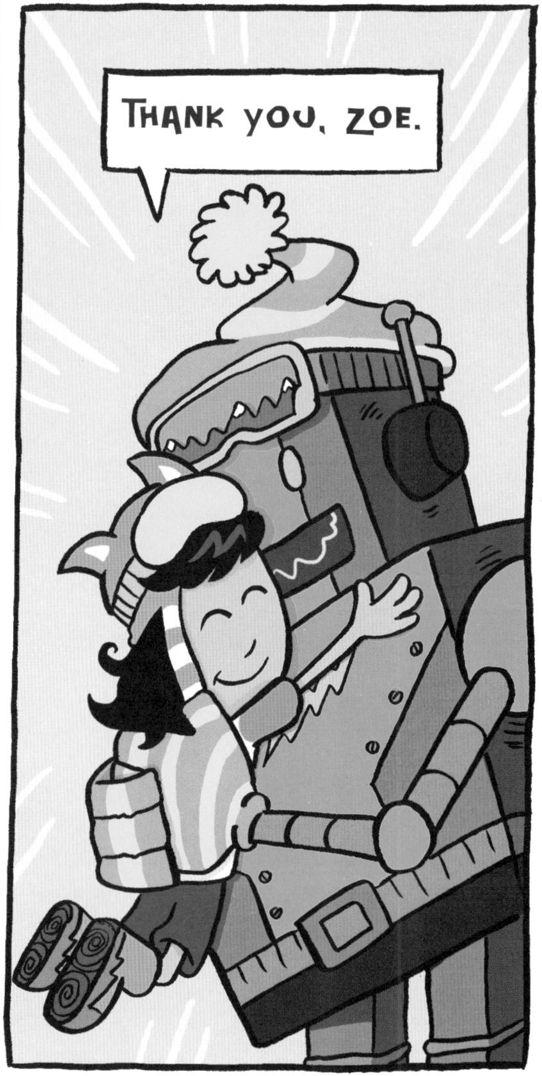
THANK YOU, ZOE.

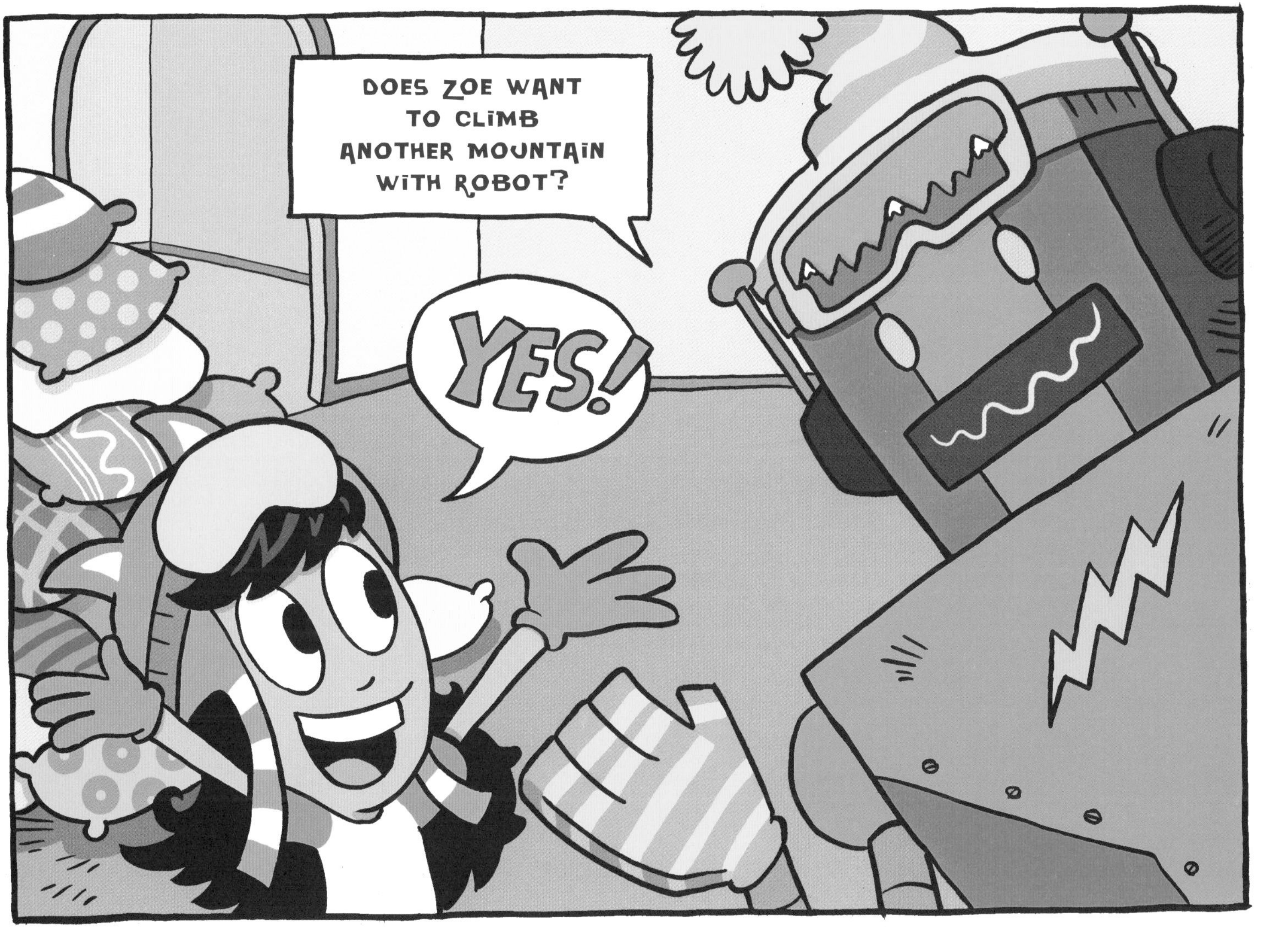
DOES ZOE WANT TO CLIMB ANOTHER MOUNTAIN WITH ROBOT?
YES!

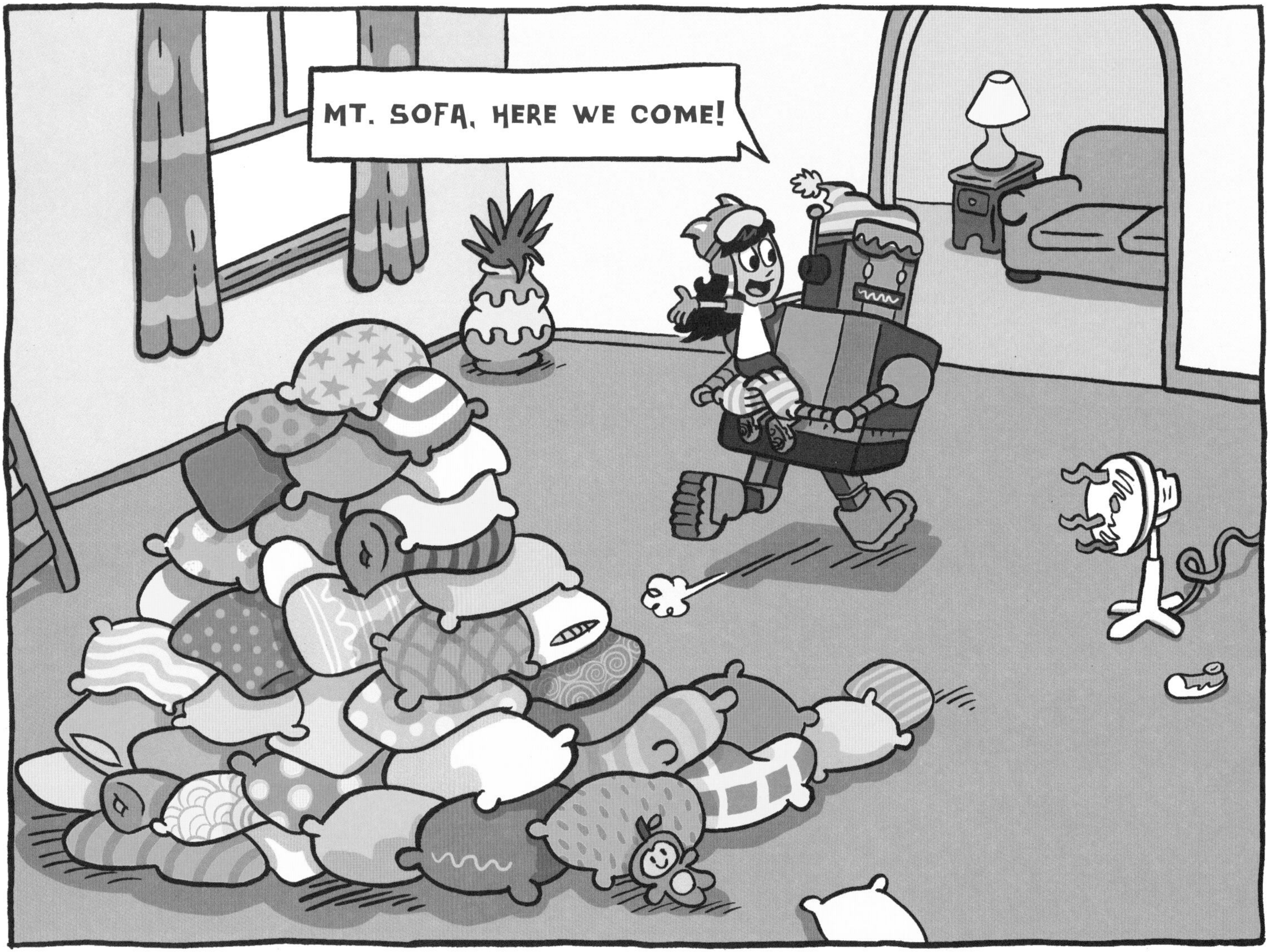
MT. SOFA, HERE WE COME!

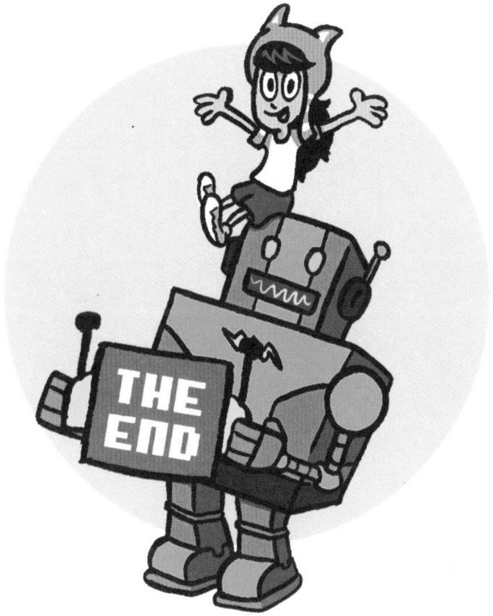
THE END

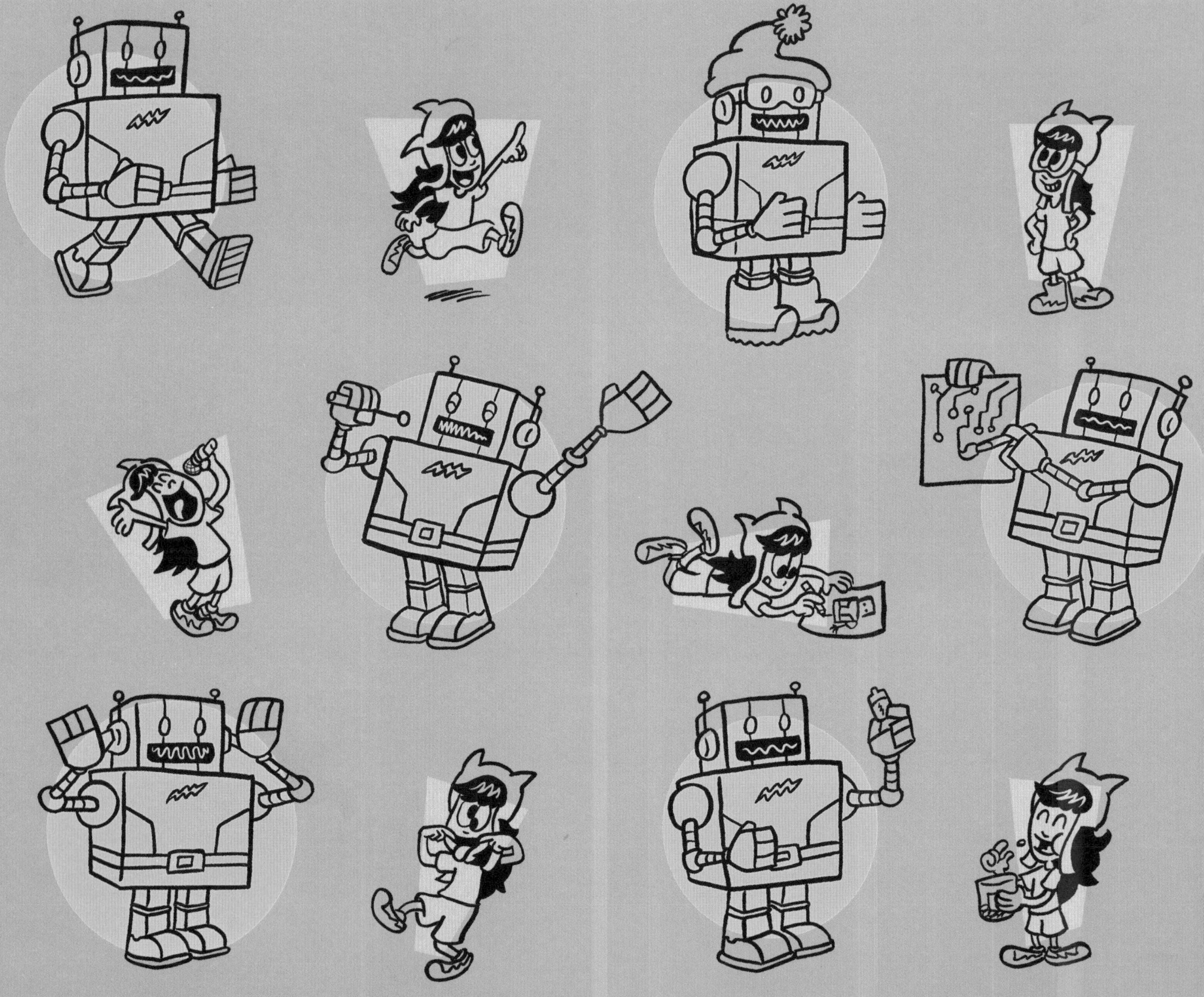